BAD HOUSES

Christopher Nosnibor

ISBN 978-1-84799-979-5

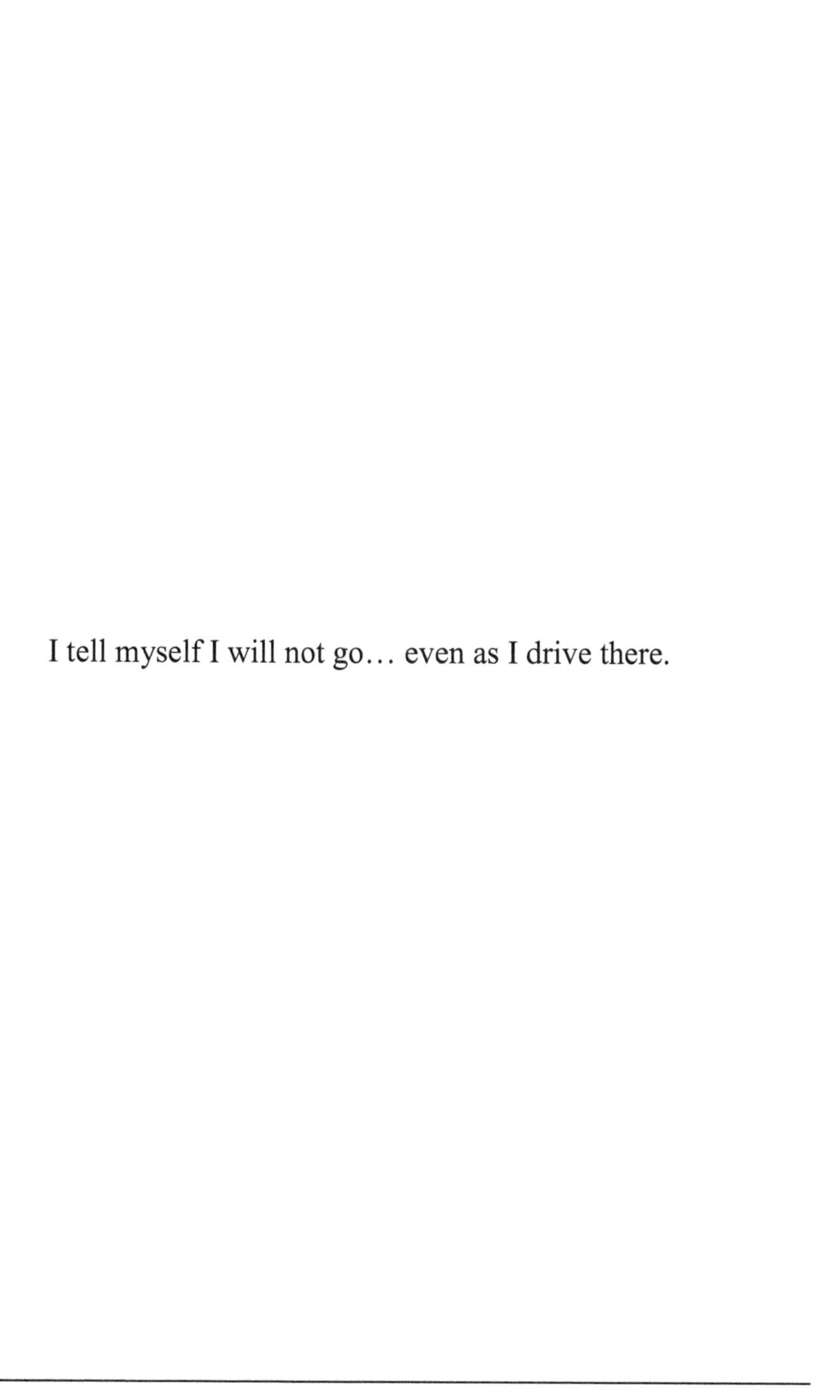

I tell myself I will not go… even as I drive there.

All persons, places and events, etc., etc., depicted herein are entirely fictional, blah, blah. Really.

A different version of ‘The House of Fit’ appeared briefly on the now-defunct website www.clinicality.org.uk. All other selections are previously unpublished.

Sections of ‘Spliced’ were produced using a number of experimental and random methods: in short, yes, it’s all intentional.

Contents

The House of Fit

I sit. The world goes on outside. I can see it through my window. Each day I observe something new. Cars pass on the road which runs in front of my home. People pass. Here on the third floor I can look down at them as they go about their business. Pretty girls; fat men, spotty youths, old women…all come and go. If I really strain to look out to the right, I can see the edge of the row of shops. From here, I cannot actually see the butcher's, post office, barber's, newsagents, grocers, chemist or chip shop. But I know they're there. They were the last time I went out.

Across the road there are houses: 1960s, two-tone semi-detached houses, as you'd probably find on the peripheries of any suburban council estate in Northern England. I see the people in tracksuits and puffer jackets go in and out, and the children with their bicycles hanging about in gangs outside on the pavement, smoking. None of this interests me all that much. But that's all there is, almost. That, my computer screen, and the house to the far left of my field of vision from my window.

The house on the far left is at an angle different from the rest, as it is on the corner of a road which turns off at right angles to the road on which I live. Like all the others, it is a typical, low-budget property, a semi-detached house constructed in the 1960s. The garden, which is little more than an unkempt lawn, furnished with skeletal push bikes and a few loose bricks, is contained by a poorly-sculpted box hedge.

The house itself, and its slightly overgrown grounds, is as uninteresting as the rest of my visible world. However, the house over in the far left of my window vista is home to a bizarre miscellany of individuals. All day, they come and go. They always emerge in groups of two or three, sometimes four. They always make only very brief excursions. And they are all females, and attractive, too. None is over the age of, say, twenty-five or so, either.

The near-constant flow of fit female traffic to and from the House of Fit, as I have come to know it, fuels hours of thoughtful musings and idle conjecture.

Could it be that the House of Fit is a knocking shop? The girls' attire wouldn't rule this out as a possibility. They come and they go, though probably with no thought of Michelangelo. But come and go they do, dressed in short skirts and tight t-shirts, or long, flowing skirts with thigh-high splits and low-cut Lycra vests. Even on the coldest, dampest days in the heart of November. The icy northern winter blast occasioned the donning of the regulation Adidas hooded tops, but the rest of the year it's clubwear and platform heals.

But what about the age of the girls? There must be about 20 or so girls, and while most look to be in the 18-25 age bracket, about half a dozen of them look to be in the 13-16 range. Well, I guess it takes all sorts.

"How much, then, luv?"

"£20."

"Few Mars bars, a Twix and some penny chews do yer to do yer?"

"Okay, granddad, if you'll crash us a fag 'n' all…"

Sometimes I sit and fantasize about the unlikely event of a contingent from the House of Fit calling around to my abode and entertaining me, individually, collectively…why? What could possibly bring them here?

"Hello, yes, good morning, we're from across the road and our washer has broken. Could we possibly impose to borrow yours?" Unlikely – it was a northern council estate periphery, after all. Fags 'n' chuddy, "'Ere, can us use yer washer? Our is bust, like, y'knerr?"

"By all means, do come in. Cup of tea? Earl Grey?"

"I aren't bothered."

"Me neiver…"

"Spare us a fag, yo?"

Not the world's greatest turn-on. But maybe I'm misjudging them. If only the girls from the House of Fit would make the journey to the shops at the top of the street, the ones just beyond my field of vision to the right…but alas, their every journey sees them turn out and head to their own right, out of the extreme left of my view, or over the road to the house opposite, also out of view. If only they'd make a trip which necessitated their passing my window, enabling me to perhaps hear their voices and take a proper look at them…

I'm lost in thought as a young girl in a low-cut white vest top hoves into range on the near-side of the road to my right. I lean forward, forehead to the glass. She passes beneath me and I draw breath …and then she is gone, out of range.

It's growing dark. I draw the curtains and move away from the window. My view of the House of Fit is fading under twilight's last gleamings. I move into the next room and turn on the computer. There's a world outside. I can see it from my windows. The large window at the front gives me access to my immediate world. But the greatest wealth of world can be found through the small window, my computer monitor. I sign on and see the world outside.

There's no need for me to go out there, other than on occasions when I need food, but dried food and tins have very long shelf lives. I can see the world outside. I don't need to go there. I don't want to go there. It's dangerous outside.

I have my life. I have my windows. I have my commodities. I have all the products I need to sustain myself in safety and comfort. I myself am a product. I am a product of the modern age. I have embraced technology and the aesthetic of the present. I have become. I have no need to socialize in the world outside – I have all the interaction I need here. I get all the world I need pumped through my windows on the world. I get all I need. I don't need more. I don't want more. I couldn't cope with more. This is the world now. And this is me. I am the ultimate product. I represent human evolution.

I have no form beyond my arms which are necessary to control the keyboard and draw the curtains. My eyes are large and lidless. I cannot blink. Blinking takes seconds out, I may miss something. I can't afford to miss a thing. I need to see everything. I need a constant inflow of information. I do not sleep. I have evolved. I am the highest form of life. I saw it all from my windows to the world outside.

Party Hard

"You gotta come, Chris," François had enthused at our last meeting. Yeah, yeah. I really wasn't the big party type, and had become even less of a party-fiend since joining the ranks of those sans employment. I suppose it has a lot to do with the fact that people always seem to define themselves in terms of their occupation.

'Hi, I'm Craig, and I'm an accountant.'

(Through gritted teeth and false, forced plastic smile) 'Pleased to meet you' **Yawn** *You dull, boring, tedious bastard, get a life.*

'Hi there, my name's Jeremy. I'm a gynaecologist. And what do you do?' *Run like hell, and don't shake his hand.*

Having no occupation somehow removes the individual from society. 'I'm unemployed,' is an instant conversation killer. 'Ah, lots of leisure time, then,' is the standard return. That's right. I have no job, and so I whittle away my days doing precisely fuck all, sleeping in until midday, then loafing about watching old films and repeats of Wheel of Fortune while drinking cups of No-Frills tea and wearing a stained dressing gown and some charity shop slippers. Yes, I'm a sponger. I love it. You get up at 6.30 every morning, and have to put on a shirt and tie before driving off in your expensive car to your big office and coming home after a hard day's telephoning people to earn a living, while I live off the taxes you pay from your hard-earned wage. Like fun. Job Seeker's Allowance is barely adequate for sustaining a half-decent healthy balanced diet – how anyone's supposed to afford to make telephone calls or buy clothes, postage stamps or bus tickets to apply for jobs or get to interviews isn't even worth contemplating. Sure, working for the Man is no gas, but at least it gives a person the means to sustain some kind of existence, and some sense of being a part of society. It also means that one has something to say when introduced to another guest at a party. So, accountancy's dull, but at least 'I'm an accountant' paves the way for an icebreaking response, which is more likely than not to refer to sailing on the accountant-sea. Of course, I always had the 'I used to work in finance, but was sacked for gross negligence,' line, but that was either going to invite an all-out interrogation which would entail, more or less, the provision of my entire life story for anything to make sense, or to send any potential conversationalist running for the kitchen. I really couldn't win. My esteem was low, and a housewarming really didn't look like my idea of fun at this point.

However, I never like to let any friends of mine down, and François had historically been a good, consistent friend to me. Besides, he had some interesting friends. Many times I had been down the pub to meet François to find he'd brought along a mate or two. Initially apprehensive by nature, I almost invariably found myself warming to his other associates, and usually found myself actually having a good time, characterised by engaging, intelligent, stimulating conversation and large quantities of Guinness being poured down my impoverished neck by Fran, who was unstintingly generous with rounds.

Unable to rustle up any remotely convincing excuses, I had graciously accepted his invitation, reminding myself that I didn't get out much, didn't get invited out much, and may, just may, get to talk to some decent folks. Failing that, I'd still be able to down a couple of firkins of ale and get a decent night's sleep afterwards. Or so I'd told myself.

Saturday came around, and I found I was quite looking forward to the prospect of a night out – something different, if nothing else. It would sure as hell beat staring at the walls, poised to pick up the phone to take calls for Janice, my flatmate, or otherwise have her calling, asking if anyone had rung for her, and have to listen to the 'are you alright, are you eating, are you keeping the flat tidy?' routine. I texted Fran at about lunchtime to ask what time I should arrive, or, more specifically, whenabouts everyone else was due to arrive. 'Any time after 8,' came the reply. Cool. I had about four hours to find some socks and boxers that didn't have holes in. I even had time to darn if necessary.

I elected to avoid any activity which would entail my engaging with people and society for the rest of the day. Shopping on a Saturday invariably riled me beyond coherent expression, and I felt as though I should conserve my sociability juices for more worthwhile encounters, such as those I hoped would be made that evening. So I pottered about the flat, did a spot of cleaning, rustled up a decent meal (my first in about eight days) in order that my stomach might be suitably lined and consequently equipped to deal with any quantity of alcoholic imbibement in which I may choose to partake, and read a few old copies of *Record Collector* magazine. Somewhere beneath the surface lay ripples of unease. I was, one could say, subliminally aware that my preparatory activities were ludicrous and as facile as… well, any other facile activity. Was I really getting excited about a party? No, of course not. I just had nothing else to do. With this knowledge lurking in the further recesses of my mind, I set about deciding what I should wear. Had I really stooped this low? Who the hell did I think I was, Bridget Jones?

At around 5pm, having checked the full-time football scores (again, not because I have any particular interest in football, but because checking the scores is another activity which fills my time), I took a shower. I washed my hair. I shaved. I applied deodorant, aftershave. I donned my rather worn (but not stained) toweling dressing gown and headed into the kitchen, wherein to fix myself a large vodka, neat.

I took it quick, took it neat, did it again.... did it again. I soon remembered that I lacked the aptitude for killing time, and so headed into town with a view to sinking a few pints and observing... merely observing. Take me out tonight... because I want to see people and I want to see life. I spent the next few hours in some dogawful student bar on the outskirts of town.

I had had just three pints of diluted bitter and left in a state of angst. I had hoped to catch a vibe, regain a sense of excitement. I had spent weeks, months, yearning for something positive, to feel that there were other people out there with ideas, other people who cared, other people who had a sense of wonder, who were motivated by a thirst for knowledge, driven by a desire to learn. More than simply this, I had yearned to find a sense of community. Recalling the hours, days, weeks I had spent in various dingy halls of residence, grotty rented low-grade accommodation and sitting around tables in countless pubs, their names and locations long forgotten, spouting, ranting and discussing, well, everything, I had made my way to the Butt and Bile, a pseudo-traditional pub in the McInterpretation of the English style. Basically, it was part of an English chain that had spread North of the border, indubitably intended to cash in on English students and no-life English nothings like me who wanted to feel as though they were still at home. With a bar full of electric pumps serving Tennent's Lager, Tennent's Velvet, Belhaven Best and Guinness Extra Cold, it felt fuck all like 'home,' but it was the closest I was likely to get.

By the time I had purchased a pint of Best at a bargain-basement £1.75 and found myself a seat at a sticky dark wood faux-mahogany table in a not-so-dark corner, I had realized that I had been a fool to expect anything of the sort I had been expecting. I had been expecting groups of young people in charity shop apparel drinking ale and engrossed in lively debates concerning all manner of intellectual perplexions and academic discourses. I had been expecting clusters of thinkers discussing the merits of the latest, most current of current affairs and the latest in a series of attacks on young women in the

Headingley area of Leeds. Police are still combing the area for possible clues, and are keen for any witnesses to come forward. The latest attack comes just three weeks after a jogger discovered the remains of an as-yet unidentified woman who appears to have been sexually assaulted and strangled before her body was burned and then discarded in a park. I had of course been expecting some inane conversation, but I had similarly expected this to be illuminated by witty riposte, however alcoholically misguided.

Instead, I had found myself once again in the company of a braying bunch of twatscamming dunces. Dressed in Levi's twisted jeans, cargo pants and other haute couture examples of urban chic, accessorised with fcuk T-shirts, Firetrap shirts, Nike hoodies and a multitude of different zip-fronted fleece type garments with 2 or 3 letters either idea of the zip which spelt something pointless like CU-BA, ITA-LIA or BOS-TON, places they'd probably never been (why not something appropriate, like TA-RT, TW-AT, CU-NT, WAN-KER, FUK-WIT?), they drank imported 'export-strength' and 'continental' lagers – Budweiser, Stella and Fosters Ice – all brewed under license in the UK – and fashionable drinks marketed at fat walleted fuckheads like them: Bacardi Breezers, Smirnoff Ice, WKD, even some fcuking schnapps-style pop-piss. They were talking about very little of any real consequence; Premiership football, the latest box-office smashing, special f-x laden, no-plot, bollock-all meaningful dialogue Hollywood feelgood films, the latest ringtones on their small-as-a-matchbox, picture email and video-messaging, all-singing, all-dancing mobile phones, new jeans, new trainers, anything but anything of import. Even the music-related discussions tended to focus on purchasing the latest new releases from Fopp, rather than the musical or lyrical merits of X, Y or Z, or the production techniques employed by anyone who was worth actually listening to. Fuck The Strokes, fuck The Hives, fuck The Vines, The Music, The Hiss, The Streets, The Faints, The Kills, The Thrills, The Chills, The Spills, The Gills, The Yeah Yeah Yeahs, The Checks, The Other, The Muffs, The Quims, The Gash, The Balls, The Knobs, The Tits, The Cunts, The Shits, The Shirts, The Farce, The Face and The Arse. And Fcuk The White Stripes, Electric Six, Electric Soft Parade, The Feeling, Orson, Razorlight, The Kooks, The Delgados, Travis, The Dull Historical Society, Aereogramme... fuck the fucking lot the of the turgid hi-trend low-merit no-mark bands. Bollocks, the fucking lot of them in their own ways.

As I leaned at the bar, waiting for my second pint to be pulled, there was a gap in the flow of tedious, self-indulgent meandering cack that was drifting insipidly from the speakers. I glanced round toward the jukebox. The barmaid was still drawing my drink from the tap. I wondered what aural seed I would hear next. A baggy-jeaned bu'fu' lolled up to the machine and bunged in a handful of coins. The 'box clocked into action and another top choice CD spun into action. I suspected that 90%, possibly more, of the people in the pub had ever even seen a 7" single, let alone owned one. The Stone Roses' 'I Am the Resurrection' started wafting out over the airwaves and began to mingle with the pall of Marlboro Light smoke that hung in the cavernous, high-ceilinged room. Too young to remember 'Sally Cinnamon,' 'I Wanna Be Adored' or 'Fool's Gold,' no doubt. Not that they'd exactly missed out. I realized that the people in whose company I found myself were of the age where even 'I Am The Resurrection' would have been something they'd heard their elder brother playing when they got home from school. And they really had no interest in looking further than the end of their nose or the NME, that pitiful rag that hung like a bogey from the end of those noses that they still needed their parents to wipe.

And so it came to pass that they didn't give a toss about the innovative production techniques Martin Hannett employed in the recording of Joy Division's *Unknown Pleasures*, the recording of each drum in the kit individually in order to create that sense of space; didn't give a shit about the fact that all the real garage music they could ever need to hear without having to subject themselves to all the lame retrograde arse of the Hives, et al, was collected on the Pebbles series of albums; didn't even know about all of the ground-breaking music of the punk, New Wave and No-Wave 'movements'...

As I made my way down my second and third pints, a cloud of gloom began to build over me.

Something shit by Something Corporate came on and it was time to leave.

****

I took the train one stop further into town, and alighted in the city centre. Upon my arrival, the realization hit that, finances and misanthropy aside, there is a very good reason why I make a point of avoiding town on Friday and Saturday nights, and that reason is everyone else. I had to virtually wrestle my way out of the station and down the street, so clogged with pre-club clubbers was the centre of the city. They made me feel old, but oh-so-wise. Very few of them seemed comfortable in their clothes – or bodies. The males, bedecked in bright shirts and shiney shoes, could readily be divided into two distinct categories: puppy fat babyfaces and lanky lean, gangling oiks with pustule-ridden complexions. The females, likewise, and one and all of the females were dressed as though in surprise at a sudden spurt of growth which had occurred at such an expedited rate that they had not had the opportunity to purchase clothing within their age range, and were, consequently, left with no option but to hit the town in their age 8-9 clothes. The newly acquired length in their arms, legs and torsos meant that skirts, only last week knee-length, barely scraped the bottom of buttocks, and that thighs, lean and sinewy, were on full display, along with pale, taut midriffs adorned with faux body jewellery about the navel. The less 'fortunate,' and I use the term advisedly, had only outward growth to adjust to, as spare tyres of rippling flesh burst forth from the space between elasticated hipster jeans and children's-sized short t-shirts; rolls of belly and blobs of overspilling back-cleavage, which at least ensured well-insulated kidneys, were complimented by 3-inch hoop earrings in gold plate and whole cans of ozone-devouring superset hair lacquer applied to home-set perms.

There were large clusters of 'alt-rockers' littering the streets, beside. Pseud skaters, dressed in jeans so voluminous that any actual skating was a physical impossibility, and hooded sweatshirts emblazoned with slogans and logos of generic, derivative sports-metal, nu-metal, no-brained neo-punkpop noisy shit that's all been done before and been done better a million times over as far back as fifteen years ago milled about aimlessly. What short memories they have. What an infinitesimally small sense of history they possess.

Queues were already forming outside pubs and clubs as I darted like a shadow through the bustling nocturnal streets. The night was young, as were the punters, but already an ugly hue was beginning to colour the atmosphere. It was the kind of ugliness that comes from people who can't hold their drink drinking excessively and being driven into excessively close proximity with one another. Tense. Or was that just me?

I was finding that as I grew older, I was becoming increasingly nervous in my disposition. This was the toll life was taking on me. My time out of employment seemed to be exacerbating the problem, my discomfiture in social settings was growing with ever swifter rapidity, snowballing in the most alarming fashion. And yet, and yet, at the same time, my desire to shrink to nothing and to hide away was countered by an insatiable curiosity, which was, I suppose, almost child-like. I believed this eternal fascination to be one of my better qualities, although it had a way of annoying the fuck out of many of my close friends, many of whom were not so close any more, or, in some cases, not so much my friends any more. Time in my company had wearied them. Like the fraught parent, sick of their child forever asking 'why?' they had reached the point of complete and utter desperation. Something had to give. Unlike the quizzical child, my tireless questioning of reason, justification and authority was not a passing phase, and therefore the only escape from the 'why' train was distance from me. What was their problem, though, really? Did they genuinely have no concern or interest in how or why things happen? On occasion, I felt as though I had grown as sick of their disinterest as they had in my curiosity. Damn, they were all so feeble. What were they whinging about? Problem was, they didn't really whinge, they merely accepted. They were essentially dead, and that rankled. I guess it doesn't do to tax the brain, to think too hard or too deep. Might uncover something ugly. The brain is like a muscle, and to overwork it would be to risk wearing it out or inducing unnecessary fatigue. Better to stick to a safe, mundane diet of cornflakes and white bread, mild cheddar and Nescafé regular than to chew a hunk of wholesome granary, tang the tastebuds with Cambizola and zap the senses with a rich, dark Java.

It's strange how the mind works. This thought struck me, not for the first time, as I continued to weave my way through the youthful rabble, and the slightly older rabble who really ought to have known better. Men in their late thirties and women in their… well, it was hard to gauge, especially with all that makeup on and under such lighting, but those lambs were truly only fit for haggis mutton, if they could only see it.

I was tense as I sliced my way through the crowds cluttering the street. Not knowing the exact location of François' new abode only served to exacerbate my agitation. I pulled the scratty yellow Post-It from my jacket pocket. By my reckoning, I was just one block away from François' posh new drum. My reckoning was right. I rang the buzzer. No reply. Given the booming bass thumps and rising voices which were pummelling the night air through an open window two floors up, which I surmised was François' place, the lack of response to my buzzing came as no surprise. I waited a minute, a minute and a half, then gave another long, aggressive prod on the button. This time, a few seconds elapsed before I was greeted with a peel of mic feedback and a distorted gabble of party noise. I tried to speak into the intercom, but this was unnecessary; the door buzzed and I pushed to find it had electronically unlatched and so I entered.

The hallway was quite remarkable. A huge, marble-lined foyer, beset by mock-Corinthian pillars to which large ornamental vines clung and the foliage of downward-hanging plants draped from in cascades was the setting in which the staircase of white alabaster with inlayed golden trim, a full eight feet wide, swept upwards toward the apartments. Such opulence I more readily associated with mansions, hotels and the type of places diplomats and people with not just money but power, the kind of power an unemployed aspiring writer could barely begin to comprehend, entertained and spent their time in tuxedos smoking rare Cuban cigars, than the type of place a twenty-six year old clinical geneticist with bad teeth and a cheap anorak may reside in. But what the fuck did I know? Shunning the lifts, I cautiously began to shuffle up the stairs clutching the carrier bag containing the £3.49 bottle of 'bottled specially for Safeway' Chilean red at 13.5% ABV. I had the feeling that it ran the risk of looking a little out of place with the other drinks if the architecture was any measure of anything. As I made my nervous ascent, I began to struggle to reconcile the idea of François at home and the François I knew, François down the pub spilling his beer as he waved his hands, dirty with newsprint and nicotine. The fear of the unknown began to envelop me as I drew nearer the Sound of the Crowd. I reached the hallway on the second floor. It was lined with subtly-located white halogen lights which were subtly hidden in architecturally-designed recesses to give a crisp, clean airy feel to the sub-atria. Two doors, wide and made of some strange set resinous compound, radiated off this atrium. Deciding which of the doors I should go through to enter François' apartment was easy: the door to my right was closed, while the door opposite and to my left was ajar and through the gap reverberated what felt like 10,000 decibels of pure party noise: pounding dance music, loud conversation and the general sound of a large gathering. As I approached the door to knock, the only means of entering I could conceive at this juncture, the door swung open and some guy I had never seen before greeted me with great gusto.

"Hi, hi, come in!" he thundered maniacally. He bid me enter with a sweeping gesticulation, slopping beer from the frothing bottle of Budweiser in his hand as he did so.

I nodded silently but graciously and eased myself over the threshold. Once inside, it took a moment for my eyes to adjust to the lighting. The hallway was quite dark, but sporadically illuminated by pulses of searing white and purple light which allowed me to locate a large number of human forms standing in groups, moving from one location to another, between rooms, and dancing. Immediately I felt quite lost. I shuffled further into the throng, looking for faces, or, failing that, identifiable body parts. Suddenly, I felt myself being swung round by some great force. I struggled to steady myself, and, balance regained, turned to face my host who had bounded up to greet me and almost toppLed me in his excessive display of enthusiasm.

"Chris!" he yelled at the top of his lungs. This was, of course, the only way he could make himself heard. "Come in! Mate, come an' check the place, let me give ya the guided tour!" He proceeded to lead me around the flat, which was impressive in terms of its sheer size if little else. And therein lay the most disagreeable aspect of the design of the living space: there was little else. Predominantly open-plan in layout, the living room / dining area / recessed kitchen had a combinative dimensionality of some 30'x65' – it was a veritable cavern, with floor-to-ceiling windows at one end. The plain plastered walls were painted entirely in white, that much I could tell even in the sporadic half-light and the coloured illuminations of the disco lights which had been rigged beside the breakfast bar which extended, although elevated a foot or so above, into the living area. A couple of small paintings hung on one of the longer walls. Smears of uncomplimentary colours with no form and thus by definition 'abstract,' looked as lost and misplaced as I was beginning to feel: the overall impression I formed of the place was that it was reminiscent of some characterless modern 'art' 'space,' akin to the abysmal 'Sight Beyond Sight' display into which I had had the misfortune to wander into and wonder where, exactly, the 'installations' were. "Whaddaya think?" he hollered.

Reeling at the incongruity of my own being within these surroundings, amidst countless people I didn't recognize, I wasn't really sure what I thought about anything. "It's huge!" I heard myself weltering back in feigned affirmation of actually liking where I was at. "It's like an art gallery," I added by way of needless embellishment.

François grinned and nodded vigorously, seemingly pleased with my comparison. Waving a bottle of Budweiser around animatedly as he beckoned me to follow him to another room, I wondered if he'd have seemed equally pleased if I had compared the flat to an aircraft hangar or the inside of a whale: his grin hinted that the beer in his hand was by no means his first of the evening.

"Ah... ah, you've bought... brought a ...a bottle!" he said loudly, the last word emerging as though in surprise and tripping over his words as he spoke, further hinting at his edging toward some state of inebriation. "Come through this way," he bellowed. "We're keeping all the drink in the bathroom. The guy I rent off, he's away this weekend, but has provided some supplies for tonight. So... check out the bath! He provided the ice... and two crates of Bud." Lo and behold, the bath, which was replete with gold taps and situated in the centre of a wooden-floored bathroom which must have measured at least 20 feet in both length and breadth and looked for all the world like the set for the famous 80s Cadbury's 'Flake' ad, was full of crushed ice and bottles of lager. A dresser at the edge of the room was home to an array of plastic drinking vessels, bottles of wine and spirits and bottle-opening paraphernalia. I added my feeble contribution to the stash as

François cracked open a very cold bottle of the so-called king of beers and handed it to me. “Wicked, innit?” he blasted, “Fuckin’ wicked!”

Feeling too overwhelmed to bark back over the tumult, I simply nodded and grinned with a conviction I really didn’t feel.

“Hey, Mikey!” François belted across the throbbing bathroom. “Oh yeah, toilet’s through there if you need it,” he said to me while simultaneously waving someone, presumably Mikey, over. “And there’s another in the en-suite in my room, second on the right. The room at the end on the left of the hall, that’s Stephen’s, the guy who owns the place, and I’m sharing with. That room’s out of bounds. I’ve stashed quite a bit of the furniture, a few pictures and the sideboard in there.” A tall, lean guy, clean shaven, sporting a fashionably tousled haircut, a tight red T-shirt and hipster jeans appeared before me and François. “Hey, Chris, you remember Mikey,” François weltered.

I didn’t. “I’m not sure I do,” I said.

“Surely you do! He was at my last party and at the quiz down at The Wickets a couple of weeks back...”

“I didn’t make your last party,” I reminded him. Had I even been invited? Really, it mattered not.

“Ah... anyway, well, Mikey’s a New Wave fan,” François hammered on, undeterred. “So you’ve probably got quite a bit in common. He’s also on the pull tonight. He split up with his boyfriend last week.”

“Ah,” I nodded, unsure of what appropriate remark I could make.

"Pleased to meet you," said the homosexual extending a deceptively strong hand, which I shook, conscious that my palm was shamefully clammy. "I'm gonna get smashed tonight, forget all about him and hopefully get laid," he grinned. "Is your man here yet?" he asked. This question was directed at François.

"He said he'd be here about 9 o' clock," Fran replied. "What time is it now?"

"Ten to."

"Cool. Chris, I'm gonna go mingle... help yourself to drink, I'm sure there are people here you know." And with that, François evaporated into the throng.

"Do you know everyone here?" I asked this Mikey character.

"I don't really know many people at all," he replied. "I don't even think François knows everyone here," he added, laughing. "He always makes it kind of open house when he has parties, and he always tells everyone he invites to bring their friends and invite other people along. Makes for some interesting parties..." he tailed off and drained his bottle. I made short work of mine, too, and accepted his offer of another. Nerves, displacement, agitation, unfamiliar surroundings, multitudinous factors, many of which underpinned my trepidation in the present environment all tended to quicken my drinking speed, which was never lackadaisical at the best (or worst, depending on your politic) of times. I chatted superficially with Mikey for the time it took to put away the beers. It felt like ages, but was probably but a matter of but five minutes. I took another bottle of the cold gassy stuff, while the pouf took his leave, a man on a mission, first to score, and, with any luck, after that, to score.

I found myself alone. The drinks I had consumed since my arrival had met with those I had consumed prior to my arrival and I began to feel their cumulative effect. Lighting a cigarette, I mused at the chorus line to Jona Lewie's 'You'll Always Find Me in the Kitchen at Parties...' It just wouldn't have ever been 'bathroom' would it? The implication would be one of the lightweight spewing their guts up, or the randy shagger getting it away with some drunken harlot. *Is there a male equivalent of a harlot?* I mused idly. Libertine doesn't quite have the same connotations. Male slates... slates slags and tapes... the word 'bathroom' certainly didn't conjure an image of the luxurious, if excessively lavish hall in which I found myself, smoking a Marlboro, drinking a lager and pondering in bewilderment in the midst of a mass of weekenders I'd never met.

A poseur in a powder blue linen jacket swanned in, nose aloft, fag held in some perceived affectation of rakishness, looking for someone. He peered down his nose, disdainfully twitching his Pyramidalis and Compressor nasi muscles, which accentuated his rather pronounced arterial furrows as he spoke to a few people. His body language oozed assurance and a conviction of superiority which was clearly not merited. In short, he looked like a wanker, and I was quietly pleased when he didn't approach me for any reason. But then, why would he? Skirting round a cluster of three sunbed-tanned bottle blondes in short skirts, halter-neck tops and knee-high patent leather boots, resting his hand on the buttocks of the tallest as he levered himself through a narrow gap en route to the door, he disappeared again. The temperature was beginning to rise and I considered removing my jacket, but its pockets contained everything I needed for my survival: mobile phone, cigarettes, lighter, a pen, a couple of sheets of paper torn from a spiral-bound notepad, my sunglasses... besides, where could I safely deposit it? No, I concluded I would simply have to sweat it out.

Time for another drink. If I carried on drinking 'beer' at this rate, despite my high level of perspiration, I'd soon be pissing like a horse, and once the floodgates opened, there'd be no stopping until the next afternoon, and so a switch to spirits would be prudent. Observing social etiquette, I refrained from claiming a bottle and carrying it around like a security blanket, and instead poured myself a plastic pint beaker full of Gordon's London Gin.

Should see me through the next hour or so, at least.

Fuelled, I turned to face the whirl and consider my next move, and was greatly relieved to see a face I recognised. I couldn't remember the guy's name, but with his thinning hair and high, bulbous forehead, he was distinctive in any crowd. We had met one night down the pub with François and had got on quite well; he was intelligent, articulate and generally knowledgeable, but not in a boring or boorish way. I gadged over to him.

"Alright...?" not being able to recall his name clearly put me at a disadvantage. We spoke for a few minutes about the flat, the other guests, peripheral random shit. He was clearly as uncomfortable as I was, and knew about as many of the other guests as I did. Finally, he decided to seek out our host, and once again, I was alone.

Gin in hand, I began to aimlessly ambulate about the palatial abode. For such a skank, François seemed to know, or at least be acquainted with, an awful lot of trendies. Their inane conversations reached my ears in fragments above the constant thudding of the music. I edged my way past several clusters of preening poseurs in fashionably faded jeans and designer shirts, a couple of cackles of chic and not-so-chic chicks wearing not quite enough accessorized with handbags not large enough to hold a tissue let alone a purse and a packet of condoms, and shoes with long pointy toes that meant I had to watch my step in order to avoid treading on them. Previous parties, drink, drugs, shoes, designers, jobs, football, television and other people's misfortunes... was this all they could consider?

No-one goes to a party to talk about serious stuff I had once been told, *no-one wants to listen to existential angst or rants about politics or theories about postmodernism or the human condition*. This was probably true, but therein lay the problem...

"And I was like..." *lifts hands, palms open, to shoulder level* "And he was like..." *pulls face* "and I was going..." *look of disgust* "and she was all..." *look of surprise or simulation of a blowjob* "and I was..."

"No*!" laughter like the laying of a large egg, concluded with a snort.*

"Yes!" *Clucking and trembling, mirth-ridden.*

"No" *Still incredulous, mopping eye with a poised index finger displaying perfectly manicured nails half an inch long.*

"Yes, really! So I was like… and it was all…"

"Ooh, yes," a tubby one interjects, "and he said, 'what?' so she said, 'yeah,' and he was all 'yeah?' and we were like, 'eh?' *Recollection falls flat, met with blankening faces.*

"Oh yeah, that's right, so I said 'yeah,' and he goes 'yeah?' and we were going, 'eh?' *Screws up face and gaggle collapse in gales of laughter once more.*

I ambled back into the cavernous main room in which the DJ and light show had been rigged. The guy behind the decks was talking to a couple of guys and smoking a phat J while some monotonous groove spiralled on relentlessly. Some girls were up in front of the makeshift DJ booth which consisted of a large pair of PA speakers either side of a drop-leaf table with an antique pine-effect veneer, dancing around their handbags and smoking Silk Cuts and Marlboro Lights. Two of them were fat and their arses stuck out as they waddled on their uncomfortable looking slingbacks. The third had long, straight dark hair and looked pretty good, but beside those heifers even the most average person would have done so. Everyone else stood in small huddles or were seated on one of the three or four sofas situated in the two recessed alcoves just off the main body of the vast open-plan space. I found myself a dark corner from which I could observe the proceedings and drink in peace: I didn't really have the front to initiate conversation with total strangers, and certainly not while I was still this sober.

A slender gothy-looking blonde in a fitted black dress was wandering around looking left and right in sharp, quick little movements, her eyes wide and bright. She flitted about the room as though in search of someone. He traversals brought me to within a couple of feet of where I was standing. She stopped and looked at me. I looked back at her. She looked as though she was about to say something but then checked herself.

"You look as though you've lost something... or someone," I said, fumbling with my lighter as I tried to light my next cigarette.

"Hmmm..." she looked a little bemused. Then her face brightened and she appeared to have regained the ordering of her thoughts. "You couldn't spare me a cigarette, could you?"

"Sure." Because, being unemployed and on my uppers, I could afford to smoke, and was more than well positioned to give away cigarettes. Because I'm a sucker. Most guys are when it comes to a pretty face. I offered her the open-ended packet and she took a cancer stick.

"You haven't got a light as well, have you?"

"As a matter of fact, I have." I flicked open the Zippo, sparked the flame and held the flame up toward her looming face and lit the cig for her, as though I was the embodiment of cool, in the way one only does when the effects of several units of gut-rotting, headache-inducing beer topped up with a substantial quantity of neat gin blended to the most incendiary cocktail with a gargantuan surfeit of adrenaline are starting to take hold.

"Thanks." I expected her to go merrily on her way, and was quite surprised when she actually struck up a proper conversation with me. My surprise manifested itself in flusterment and I managed to stutter and fluff my way through a few exchanges about what I can't recall. Then it came: "What is it you do?"

Fuck: a stumble at the second fence. I stammered and paused, scratched my nose and hesitated. "I'm a writer," I blustered. It was half true. To be a writer doesn't mean one has to be published: one just has to write. Writing is a vocation, a calling. Genet said of a French writer who shall remain nameless: "he does not have the courage to be a writer." What courage does he refer to? The courage of inner exploration, the cosmonaut of inner space. The writer cannot pull back from what he finds because it shocks or upsets him, or because he fears the disapproval of the reader. Right now, I had the courage, but lacked the art of articulation on account of the alcohol. Still, it seemed to work: she looked impressed.

"What sort of writing?"

"Fiction." Lame. Very lame – but suitably vague.

"Go on."

Damn. "Well, I'm not really into genre fiction," I hemmed, devising my Call for Escape Route. "Although I'm quite into intertextuality and borrowing from various sources. I guess you'd loosely call it postmodern, although that's a pretty meaningless term if you ask me." She still looked interested and as though she expected further expansion, so I continued. "I guess in simple terms it's fairly high-octane stuff, chock full of gratuitous sex and violence. And lots of swearing." I noticed she was smiling, so I smiled too. I also noticed that she had nice tits. Not big, but pert and well-proportioned. I smiled some more. She asked if I'd had anything published. "Not yet," I told her, but I said I was touting a few shorts around a few magazines and the like. This much was true. She then proceeded to tell me all about a friend of hers who was a writer, a freelancer who'd managed to get quite a few shorts published in specialist sci-fi periodicals and collections. After a while, I realised that her knowledge of the sci-fi genre was disturbingly vast. I was probably supposed to be impressed, but I wasn't. Everyone's a writer or an artist, or knows a writer or an artist, and sci-fi, the majority of it, is for sad pubescent tossers and sad tossers who never realised they'd actually stopped being pubescent. Still, at least she wasn't a horror buff. Those twats really are the worst. And Steven King's so dull. Almost as bad as Salman Rushdie, although not as much of a pseud.

'You have to give his narrative time,' someone had once told me. 'His storytelling style isn't one you can just race through. You have to persevere.'

But I had persevered: one summer, I attempted diligently to plough my way through *Midnight's Children*. Three months and 26 pages later, I had to admit defeat. I could not wade through another text of his turgid prose. But at least I had caught up on some much-needed sleep. King, I managed for a while as an impressionable teenager, before discovering the world of postmodern, non-genre fiction and realising that King was ultimately tedious. But vs. Rushdie? Close call. King has the beard.... but Rushdie has the nose, which makes the duel of the dullards a close-fought contest. It dawned on me that I really wasn't giving this girl my undivided attention and that the only reasons I'd not made any excuse to take my leave were that I couldn't think of any possible excuses or places to go and that she was incredibly pretty. But so the fuck what? She asked if I could spare her another cigarette: I obliged and the conversation rolled on, albeit somewhat one-sidedly. Eventually she decided she had to go and continue her search for Katriona or someone.

"Nice to meet you, Chris," she said.

"Likewise..." Had she even told me her name? We shook hands and she faded into the smoke and the crowd. More people were dancing now. I spotted François by the decks. He was inexpertly spinning a couple of discs, attempting to mix Ragga with some high-treble punky / garage noise, which he quickly replaced with some very pacey Drum 'n' Bass. His movements were somewhat disjointed and he looked pretty wired, from which I surmised his man had probably shown.

I kept close to the walls, surveying the scene as the party really began to swing: people were starting to look ever so slightly dishevelled, eyes wide and faces pink or puce, the temperature was rising rapidly as more bodies began to pack into the space and the volume of the music reached the magic eleven as it pounded to compete with the shouting of the conversing guests and hangers-on. On one of the sofas sat a couple of girls in their mid-twenties, dressed to the nines and with expensively-manicured false-looking nails. Their hair and makeup must've taken them hours to perfect.

"So I was saying to my counsellor, I know I have a problem with my body image, and I think it's all connected to the fact that Daddy had that affair with his secretary who used to be a model..."

I rounded on her with a snarl. I had Cruised. Now I would Force the Truth.

"Do you get what you want?

Who cares for you nowadays?

What do you think of yourself?

Do you ever say no to anybody?

How far do you let them go?

Afterwards, do you ever complain?

How long do you spend with each?

Do you know what you want?"

At this juncture it dawned on me that I was pretty pissed. Correction: I was utterly fucking gashed. I looked at these disgusting, loathsome specimens, wrapped up in their self-centred little universes, so far removed from anything that actually mattered and felt faintly nauseous: it was nothing to do with the amount I had drunk, although I noticed with slightly swimming eyes that the pint of gin was now no more than a half pint. The stick insect who was speaking had large bleached white teeth which glowed in the flashes of ultraviolet light and very prominent clavicles, accentuated by her low-cut vest top. She looked as though she'd not eaten more than a lettuce leaf, rinsed and dabbed dry and accompanied by no more than a grain of salt and a splash of light dressing in three days. Sucking on a light menthol cigarette and sipping at a gin and slimline tonic, all a part of the overall self-maintenance programme, she was surrounded by an aura of delusional egotism. Her friend / confidante / unpaid counsellor sat and nodded, sipping her insipid alcoholic fix, leaving a thick coating of Max Factor Ultimate Lipsheen color no. 48 on the rim of the plastic drinking vessel. I wanted to throttle the fucking pair of them and suffocate every last one of their friends and families, on by one, using their own pillows as they slept. Relentlessly I continued.

Perhaps you could tell us about your personal habits?

Where do you buy your groceries?

What do you buy for yourself?

What was your last meal?

What kind of toilet paper do you prefer?

Is there a song you'd like to hear?

Are you sleeping well?

Can I pour you a drink?

What are you doing about your skin?

Has sex been a way to escape your problems?

What docs scx mcan to you anyway?

Does alcohol help?

Do you feel depressed afterwards?

Do you get what you want?

What are you getting out of it?

Does it hurt you emotionally?

What are you scared of, pain?

Who can you talk to?

Are you really happy with the way you look?

What do you think of yourself?

I took another monster slug of gin and felt the liquor burn in my gullet.

Do you remember when you were young?

And was this part of the dream?

All a part of the dream... in fact I spake not a word as I slipped, unnoticed, past the pointless wastrels. Thing started to get a bit much. I was becoming somewhat dizzy and disorientated. I didn't feel right in my own skin, my flesh was hot, crawling beneath my clothes. On autopilot, I lit another cigarette. The nicotine rush only served to exacerbate my sense of a need to escape my body and shut off my mind. On a physical level, I was losing my sense of perspective: psychologically, I was simply losing my sense. Like a machine with no manual override, I continued to drink and smoke, and all the while my reactions and coordination grew progressively more impaired. I couldn't even compute the fact that I would feel like death come the morning: the concepts of morning, day, night, time had fled my functional mind. People were starting to look uncommonly ugly and there were couples who weren't actually couples, at least not yet, copping off in various corners of the room. It was time to get the hell out and make my way home. I had no idea how I would get there. Consciously I had forgotten the route and knew, somehow, that I would be reliant upon my instinct to get me back, and get me back alive. But I should really bid my host farewell first and thank him... for what precisely, I wasn't sure, but however drunk, I never forget my manners. At least not these days...

I embarked upon a mission to find François. I stumbled about, lost, in the sporadic lighting, fag hanging. No-one seemed to notice: they were all fucked on something or another. I asked a few people if they'd seen François. Those who could still speak said they hadn't seen him all that recently. I checked the bathroom and saw the guy with the large forehead in conversation with some other strange looking bloke. I gadged over and told him I was off shortly – had he seen François?

"Heading into one of the bedrooms, I think," he slurred.

"Sheeeers, mate."

I opened the first door I came to. It was crowded, full of people who looked deeply spaced and who probably made me look decidedly together by comparison. Hardly anyone moved as I threw open the door. One scrawny-looking student type did manage to lift his head.

"Ayyy... wan' some K? Fukken a...."

I declined and tried the next door. The room, a bedroom, was dimly lit. Mikey had pulled. The tart aroma of spunk and rectal mucus hung heavy in the air. Mikey was bent forward, rimming some skinny white guy who looked no more than 17. He looked up, his eyes like dead fish eyes, glazed, a fixed idiot grin plastered on his pallid drugfucked visage. While he set to beating the meat, I beat a hasty retreat and tried the next door.

At last, I found François. Another bedroom, dimly lit, the ginger fiend was facing the door and was standing over the bed. Some brunette chick with large dugs was crouched on all fours on the edge of the bed and was yelping like a Terrier as he pumped her from behind. Her eyes were rolling upwards in their sockets: François' eyes glowed blood-red in the dark, his teeth were gritted and sweat was running down his luminescent torso. He faced me as I entered with a murderous look upon his face. A second glance informed me that he was more like a man possessed, present but not present, and certainly not correct. He'd not remember my intrusion, and so I hastily closed the door. I downed the last inch of gin and left through the open door. Yet more people were entering as I slipped out.

The emptying of the glass was my downfall. The inside of my cheeks began to trickle with thick saliva and a sick sweat broke on my brow. Whiteout! I bounded down the broad mock-marble staircase in slow motion, bile rising up my alimentary canal. With precision timing, I reached the main door and the outside world. The cold air hit me like a freight train, but I didn't have a second to compose my thoughts. Everything I had consumed during the last six hours or so raced upwards and through the floodgates of my pharynx. Within a split second of making contact with the pavement I was spewing like a volcano. Regaining my senses, I realized that this megabarf would doubtless be the first of many: I wasn't going to feel too good in the morning.

You've Got It Coming

It had been a hard day at the office. *Same as any other*, Stuart reflected as he turned the key and heard the Yale's snib lift in the front door of the modest mid-terrace he rented. Nothing spectacular by any means, but it was comfortable and it was home – at least for now – the place he could go and, on a good evening, forget about the 9 to 5, kick back and do the things that pleased him. And, more importantly, the real work as he considered it: in order to supplement his rather meagre wage as a chairpounding admin prole, Stuart took as many freelance writing jobs as he possibly could. This meant he didn't get a great deal of spare time, but he found it provided an outlet for his creative 'talents' while also keeping him in food, and beer, and a roof over his head. Such things may be simple, but their importance should never be underestimated.

Cracking open his first beer of the night, a bottle of Spitfire, he decided to skip tea and get straight down to work. Having completed his last article ahead of the deadline, he was keen to crack on with a short story he had recently begun, a Sadean vignette reflecting the decline of interactive skills in the late capitalist age of greed. He took a long draught down of the hoppy ferment and allowed the various complex notes to burst over his palette whilst simultaneously slaking his raging thirst and then ascended the stairs to the study.

By far his favourite room in the house, this small South-facing room was neutrally decorated, thus allowing the natural light to illuminate the space, which contained his PC just beside the window – far enough to one side to prevent any direct sunlight causing any distraction – and was quite literally packed with books as well as an amplifier, a number of guitars, including an old electric bass with a slightly warped neck and the inlay missing from the third fret, and a selection of CDs which he liked to listen to while he worked.

Firing up the PC, he looked out of the window which overlooked the back yard and the back of the terrace of the next street. It was early spring, and the evening sun was pleasant to behold: from indoors, the fact that this early sun contained little heat was immaterial. It looked nice and made Stuart Bateman feel pretty good. He had left his troubles at the office and had a pleasant, peaceful evening in prospect, with free time at his disposal for a change. Below, he could see the girl next door in her back yard: an artificial blonde and somewhat beefy. He winced inwardly at the sight of her shuffling to the back gate with two black bags stuffed almost to bursting, the excess flesh which kept her kidneys well insulated overhanging the low-riding waist of her distressed size 14 hipster jeans. The fact she was a rather generous size 16 was not lost on Stuart, who felt a mild wave of revulsion wash over him when she bent to put down the bags and open the gate and a high-riding fuchsia pink thong hoved into view. The computer was now booted and so Stuart set to work, taking occasional sips from his pint and casually observing his neighbour's activities as she made frequent journeys to the back gate with more and more black sacks and cardboard boxes. Putting it down to a vigorous Spring clean, Bateman soon forgot about what he had seen and immersed himself in his writing whilst carried away by the bottom-heavy guitar sludge of Fudge Tunnel's *Hate Songs in E Minor*. Stopping only to get more beer and to urinate every hour or two, he worked late into the night. Tomorrow was Friday, and frankly, he didn't give a fuck. He could do his job in his sleep anyway, and suspected a retarded chimp could probably do likewise.

He awoke feeling fresh the following morning: the sun was out and filled the embittered churl with an uncharacteristic *joie de vivre*, doubtless accentuated by his spate of literary productivity the previous night. The day passed without event and Stuart left the office raring to get back to his short story, which he had now given the working title 'Try And Be Grateful' after the Whitehouse track. As he unlocked his front door, just as he had the previous evening and countless evenings previous, he noticed the 'To Let' sign screwed to the wall of the house next door. He worked with the curtain open after dark that night, and, sure enough, the windows next door remained in darkness until he retired at 3 am, his story almost complete.

A week later, Stuart returned home after a gruelling and exhausting week at The Corporation, tired and stressed and with a tight deadline. He had until 9am Monday morning to produce and submit 5,000 words on nostalgia. It was only earning him seventy quid, but he had an angle and had been warming to the subject as he had contemplated and researched the piece, which would focus on the way in which it is a natural tendency to hark back to the decade in which one grew up as a 'golden age' in comparison to the bleaker present. Thus, children of the fifties complained about the epidemic of moral decline which characterised the sixties, decade of free love; while children of the seventies spent the eighties mourning the loss of 'real' music as the synthesiser became the instrument of choice. Etc.. But Stuart was coming to the conclusion that while every decade's children yearned for 'their' decade, having rose-tinted it as somehow 'better,' the present was by far the worst time to be alive. He was too tired to work tonight: having spent almost eight hours straight in front of a monitor at the office, his eyes were strained and he was experiencing difficulty focussing. He had a cranium-shredding headache. He needed a drink. It had been a hard day at the office. Same as any other, Stuart reflected as he turned the key and heard the Yale's snib lift in the front door of the modest mid-terrace he rented. Before he crossed the threshold, he noticed the 'To Let' sign now had 'Let' plastered over it, and began to wonder what the new tenants would be like.

He didn't have long to wait. Despite having consumed four bottles of strong ale – including one of Theakston's Old Peculier at a robust 5.7% ABV and one of Marston's Strong Pale Ale which weighed in at a dizzying 6.2% ABV – followed by considerable quantities of unbranded vodka, in an attempt to obliterate all thoughts of The Corporation, Stuart awoke at first light to the sound of blackbirds chelping from the chimneys and aerials along the terrace feeling pretty sharp. He showered and dressed and made a pot of Earl

Grey and was ready to get to work by 9.30 am. It was a little more than half an hour later when he heard shuffling and thudding sounds through the walls coming from the vacant property next door. Breaking from the article and moving to the bedroom, he gently pulled aside the mandatory net curtain to see a car parked outside on the street below. A slightly spotty youth in baggy jeans, a baseball cap and a Nike hoodie was at the boot of the car, lifting a black sack, straining and full, from which the leg of a pair of tracksuit bottoms with twin parallel lines down the seam hung limply from the top, from the vehicle. He disappeared into the next terrace and was replaced by another, almost identical youth in an ADIDAS hoodie and red baseball cap. At 27, Bateman figured these punks were probably almost a decade younger than he. And he felt old. Very fucking old.

At eleven, Stuart took a break. He was already 1,500 words into the article and it was evolving nicely. He ate a packet of crisps and cracked open a can of Scrumpy Jack. Although he usually only drank cider in the summer, the pleasant Spring weather had embedded within him a Summery vibe, and a drink always aided his writing. Yes, it was only 11 am, but Stuart's rule of alcohol consumption ran thus: 'are the pubs open? Yes? Then it's ok to drink. No? Then why aren't they open? It's time for a drink...' Given that a number of Wetherspoons had recently taken to serving alcoholic beverages from 8.30 am provided a meal, i.e. breakfast was also purchased, this rule was usually covered by Regulation One, although a packet of crisps would not, to the minds of most, necessarily constitute a meal. Stuart wasn't bothered. He had a job to do, and a drink or two were integral to his performance. From next door, the strains of some crappy Nu-

Metal shouting and grating abortion filtered through the wall, but this was not going to slow his rapidly-paced typing as he tapped keys in flurries in time with the solid rhythms of Fields of the Nephilim's *Fallen* album.

Whatever the faults of these preceding decades, they were still better than the present. History has a habit of repeating itself. The only trouble is, with each repetition, the concentrations of shit and poison become greater, like toxins being passed down the food chain.

Stuart thrashed out a sound conclusion to his article to the album's pounding closer, 'One More Nightmare (Trees Come Down AD).' What it lacked in terms of the 1985 original's atmosphere, it more than compensated in sheer power and sinister vocal distortion, while presently, what the article lacked in length, it compensated in ideas and quality of prose.

This dying age…

This dying age…

This dying age…

By the end of Saturday, he had a good working draft down, and so he decided to treat himself to a lie-in on Sunday morning, before going shopping for his weekly groceries prior to resuming work. After all, he only had 1,000 words left plus editing to finish the piece, and a full day plus evening in which to yield his quota. No sweat! It was another nice day, and so Stuart took his time walking to and from the supermarket. But the niceness of the day was shattered on his return home by the earth – and wall- shaking racket which was vibrating the very foundations of the modest mid-terrace he rented. Music. Well, instruments. Played badly, and at high volume. The sound filled the street outside his front door, and the volume grew exponentially as he entered his rented haven. He put away the shopping as the drums, pummelled erratically and arhythmically but with considerable gusto, filled the little kitchen. The guitar, thick with distortion but thoroughly lacking in tone or tune, pierced the mortar and weighted the air in the living room.

Having decanted the contents of a bottle of Waggledance into a glass, with some trepidation, Stuart headed up to the study. Holy fuck! The racket was unbearable as the floor beneath his feet shuddered: the rehearsal room was directly next to his study! He couldn't hear a thing, let alone a thing as quiet as a thought in there, and the bedroom was little better. At full tilt, he could just about hear the television. It being a Sunday, there was nothing worth watching on, but this, the writer reflected, was not the point. Still, he fired up the PC and attempted some work, but without success. Stuart's writing process involved the formulation of words and sentences in his mind's ear: that is to say, while he didn't speak aloud while typing, he recited the words in his head as he typed and could feel their flow. All he could hear as he sat before the keyboard on that afternoon was the unholy whorle of sound puncturing the airwaves through the walls to his right. Playing his own music didn't help, as this only added to the cacophonous mesh of noise and floor-shuddering bass guitar and drum, all played out of sync with one another. It was fucking horrible, and as a last resort, Stewart decided to take a walk. Anywhere. Just out.

On returning an hour later, he could hear the same dreadful din three streets away: standing in the back yard, he realised that the adolescent nu-metal bozos had the window to the rear upstairs room open as wide as it would go. Fucking idiots. The racket persisted throughout the day, during which time Stuart wrestled with the idea of going round and asking them to turn it down – rather hard to turn down a drum kit, he concluded, giving his new neighbours the benefit of the doubt that it was probably a one-off – and finally desisted at 10.30. At this point, Stuart, tired and fraught and headache-troubled and rather full of beer set to finishing his article, which he finally emailed off at 3.15 am. Four hours sleep then up for work, he thought. Bad start to the week.

With another article demanding his attention on his return home from work on Monday night, Stuart was dismayed to arrive at the modest mid-terrace to find the teenage dirtbags were rehearsing again. Rehearsing what, precisely? They had no songs and rarely played so much as a couple of bars as a coherent collective, preferring instead to bludgeon away at their own things independently of one another, but simultaneously. Stuart considered himself a music fan, but even to his tolerant ear – he found Truman's Water a challenging but enjoyable listen – they were less unified than Captain Beefheart and his not-so-magic band on *Trout Mask Replica* which Stuart thought sounded like seven people playing seven different songs in different keys and in different time signatures in separate rooms of the same house.

Unable to settle to work, he wandered about the modest mid-terrace but was unable to escape the thundering clatter of out-of-time, nine beats to the bar, 11/8 signature drums which followed the striking of the chords on the nearly-in-tune bottom-heavy distorted guitar. The drummer is supposed to set the rhythm! Although in order to do this, it was necessary for the drummer to possess a sense of rhythm… the drumming stuttered over an interminable floor-tom fill and the guitar faltered before it halted, its sustain lost in a squeal of poorly-earthed feedback. Seconds later, the noise resumed again. The study, the place where concentration was required, was by far the worst affected room: the floorboards beneath his feet, upon which his chair stood, shook under the burden of the throbbing racket. The bedroom, next to the study, situated to the front of the house, was only marginally better as the sound and vibrations still shook the dividing wall which separated the two properties. Downstairs, the living room, which occupied the entirety of the ground floor and corresponded to the plan of the study and bedroom, and was thus a large space indeed, suffered from the noise and vibrations coming down through the floorboards and again through the brickwork. Stuart could only conclude that the vibrations in the upstairs rooms resonated through the building's very fabric, which served to act as an amplifier into his own space. It was a conclusion which did not please him one bit. He gave up on his attempts to watch television, as it was necessary to turn the set up to a volume which made his head ache simply to hear a word that was being said. He tried the back yard, but that was even more badly affected than the study, because the little fuckers had the window to the room in which they were playing open as wide as it would go.

This was most definitely a spirits night. Stuart had work to do, had had a tough day at work and he was in no mood for this. Pouring a good three-fingers measure of generic, unbranded vodka, he began to consider his options. He could, in theory, go round there and knock on the door, asking them politely if they'd mind keeping it down. Next door's front door was only five feet to the left of his own. But that would be pointless. They'd not hear him knocking. And if they did, then what? One can't turn a drum kit down, especially if one hadn't even mastered the playing of the thing yet. So he'd have to tell them to stop altogether. Which was a little dictatorial, and likely to put their backs up. Stuart was of slight build, and not very tall – a mere 5' 8" – and while he was no pussy, he was aware of the fact that there were three of them and only one of him, and while he was intellectually superior, these nu-metal bozos were probably not too slow with their fists when the supposed need arose, and wouldn't respond on level terms to any treatise on social responsibilities and the importance of consideration for others. A note through the door was an option, which Stu also rejected. Assuming they could actually read, they'd probably just rip it up and laugh, and after fifteen minutes of Beavis and Butthead snickering, resume their cacophany, tweaking the volume knobs to eleven, knowing that whoever was complaining was too chickenshit to challenge them face-to-face and that they could get away with it. A pebble to the back window? A brick? Nah, far too risky. Initiating such direct action was an open invitation for retaliation, and all-out war was not on Bateman's agenda. Environmental health was an option, but it was 6.30 at night and this was only the second incident concerning their Very Metal Noise Pollution. The cops?

Stuart thought back to his own adolescence. Despite being a law-abiding citizen, he'd had the heat round on his parents' back doorstep on two occasions; once during a particularly riotous house party he'd thrown while his parents were away, which had seen some 30-plus underage drinkers get absolutely rat-arsed and rowdy, shouting and playing music until after midnight. It must've been fairly loud, he'd reflected, as his parents had lived in a detached property with no immediate neighbours for a good thirty yards. But that had been a one-off, and even when he had formed a band, they had been careful to rehearse in the garage and to restrict both the duration and volume of their rehearsals. Substituting drummer with drum-machine had helped: it's far easier to turn one of those things down than an acoustic drum kit. And you don't need some gormless perspiring chimp to thump away at a drum machine, so it's a win-win situation. The tosser next door was serving to affirm all of Stuart's prejudices about drummers as he pummelled and clattered away, hopefully to be soon rewarded with a mug of PG, followed by a lethal injection for crimes against music. The other visit from the pigs had been in connection with a pamphlet he'd co-produced which had caused offence to someone's mother. It hadn't been addressed to her, so it really wasn't her business calling the fuzz, but they'd simply warned him not to produce any more offensive literature disguised as the local Parish News.

Deciding to show some clemency and leave calling the rozzers until he was truly at the end of his tether, Stuart poured himself another large measure of the clear spirit and reflected – or attempted to. But it was too damn loud to do anything, and he certainly couldn't work. He did, frequently, work with music on. But that was just it – the infernal din wasn't music. He paced the length of the living room a dozen or so times, vexed and perplexed by this existence-impinging predicament. He downed the drink and poured another.

And then it stopped. Stunned by the silence, Stuart glanced about; moved swiftly to the back door and opened it; stood in the back yard and looked up and the open window of the upstairs back room of the house next door; listened intently; the wind gently blew through the trees in the gardens along the terrace; their leaves rustled gently; the tunes of the throstles and blackbirds in the neighbourhood were audible. Peace was restored. The contrast between the new quietness and the previous protracted sonic boom was astounding. In shock, reeling from the change in the weather, Stuart slugged back his drink, poured yet another and went up to the study and fired up the PC: he had work to do. He wasn't really in the appropriate frame of mind, but he had a deadline to meet, and meet it he would. The cupboards were almost bare; pay-day was some way off and the fifty pounds this article would earn him meant a week's food and a couple of bottles of some potent and intoxicating liquor of his choice. Of course, if he would drink less, his money would go rather further. But a certain level of alcohol in the bloodstream served to promote his creativity, and, moreover, acted as a much-needed anaesthetic which numbed his mind and drove out the horrors of the 9-5.

He sat down and began to type, but a mere 20 minutes later a humming commenced next door in the room immediately adjacent to the study. Someone was firing up an amplifier. The customary pre-drumming rattle and sampling of each component of the kit followed: the children were playing again. And so they continued, drums, bass and guitar, all at full-throttle for another hour, during which time Stuart tried watching television; reading; reading with headphones and listening to his own music; reading with earplugs, all to no avail.

Once again, at 10p.m. on the dot, the fearsome howl abated. Stuart, tired and rather worse the wear for drink, resumed work. He wasn't happy. He really didn't appreciate having his flow broken, his rhythm – something the drummer next door was seriously lacking – disturbed. He sat at before the glaring monitor, having lost his place, the writer's greatest obstacle after writers' block. Although Stuart always found his best work – at least his best creative pieces, which 'Try and be Grateful' had all the makings of being one of – came to him in flashes of ugly, manic inspiration, he did not truly believe in the totality of writers' block. His recent experiences of set word limits and tight deadlines had led him to believe in the merits of hack work and plagiarism – to borrow and paraphrase from diffuse sources – even to copy and paste chunks from his own previous works – was not only wholly legitimate in the postmodern age, but even represented a substitute for inspiration at times when it mattered. Hell, the best and most judicious sourcing was a creative method in itself. But on this night, the words would just not come, from any source, and when they did, fitfully, disjointedly, and lacking the spark of dynamism he could feel when truly in The Zone, his fingers lacked the instinctive coordination of the times when he was on a roll, when he was in his stride, repeatedly miss-keying the simplest of words with almost unerring regularity. A muffled thrumming fed through the wall as his new neighbours got the stereo revved up with more Linkin Park and System of a Down. It wasn't nearly as bad as the live set-up, but it was nevertheless bloody irritating. Stuart poured himself a large vodka and lobbed a CD into the computer's drive. He had a word count to make up, and while this session would probably weaken the overall impact of the piece through some less than wonderful writing, Stuart decided it was time to start hacking. He let the swirling chords of the epic neo-prog Oceansize debut, *Effloresce*, wash over him and the words began to flow. But after a mere 10 minutes, bass frequencies began to vibrate the floor beneath his feet as one of the selfish children next door struck up his instrument again, inexpertly ponking random off-tune notes clumsily off the fretboard of his Encore. It wasn't quite as bad as having the full band going full throttle, so Bateman cranked up his own speakers to mask the bollocks bass-playing and did his best to ignore it.

It was another three hours before silence fell over the house next to Stuart's rented accommodation, by which time he had not only finished the article, but also the bottle of vodka. He mailed the piece off and fell into an agitated, dream-disturbed sleep, full of scenes of work, fights with adolescents in sports-metal attire and abstract alcohol-fuelled images.

Stuart awoke the following morning dying for a piss and with a sharp ache in his kidneys. His head was a little muzzy too. He checked the bedside clock. 9.05! Shit! Late for work already... as he hurried to ready himself – no time for a shave today – the strains of more heavy shit penetrated the walls; Coal Chamber, Slipknot… of course, these young punks had no idea that it had all been done before, and been done better. For schlock-horror metal, Marilyn Manson was just Alice Cooper thirty years too late. Hell, Alien Sex Fiend had also done the goth-horror thang with greater aplomb, and with better tunes, too. 'I'm Doing Time in a Maximum Security Twilight Home' and the *All Our Yesterdays* LP provided ample evidence to substantiate the opinion Stuart held. For hard and fast, forget the current crop when you could have Ministry or Skrew and if you wanted it really hard and fast, to the point of being unintelligible, there was Napalm Death or Extreme Noise Terror – the latter of whom's collaborative re-recording of '3am Eternal' with the KLF was a masterpiece. It was to the slow pounding of grindcore masters Godflesh on his Discman that Stuart headed to work that morning.

He was angered, but unsurprised, to return home to the horrible aural assault of another 'rehearsal.' However, to actually call this routine noise-making with instruments a rehearsal would be rather a misapplication of the word, for to rehearse first requires for something to have been formulated in order to be developed, learned. There was no shape to this racket, just random thrashing, trashing, bashing… and Stuart was in no mood for it. It had been a hard day at the office. Same as any other, he reflected as he turned the key and heard the Yale's snib lift in the front door of the modest mid-terrace he rented. Unable to hear the television over it, or think to read or write, Stuart fucked off down the pub to get away from it and to consider his plan of action: it was plain that he could not allow for this to persist indefinitely.

As he sat in a dark, quiet corner of his local with a pint of Black Sheep Special, he considered moving his own stereo speakers to point directly at the wall which adjoined his most annoying and inconsiderate neighbours and playing the Swans album *Cop* at full volume on a loop, or, using Einstürzende Neubauten's *Strategies Against Architectures I, II* and *III*, with its fire-extinguisher-against-shopping-trolley percussion as a sonic equivalent to water torture. Better still, a handful of Whitehouse albums back to back. From the blistering shards of pure treble feedback of the early *New Britain*, *Erector* and *Dedicated to Peter Kurten* albums, via the muted squeal of *Psychopathia Sexualis* and *Right to Kill*, through to the relentless all-out total noise of *Cruise* and *Bird Seed*, the white-noise extreme electronica of the only band that could make Throbbing Gristle sound like a lounge act would be enough to send these nu-metal loving girls running to their mummies with piss in their oversized jeans. He was aching to crank everything up to eleven for the whole duration of back-to-back playings of 'A Cunt Like You' and 'Wriggle Like a Fucking Eel.' But that would only lower him to their level, he mused, and besides, he then ran the risk of getting complaints from his neighbours – if they didn't call the police on him. He returned to the modest mid-terrace after drinking up time, having drunk up four or five pints of real ale. The dull thrum of wall-to-wall metal shit buzzed in the bedroom as he lay in bed, unable to sleep.

Stuart let his mind wander and as he lay somewhere between inebriation and sleep, visualised himself vaulting the wall into his neighbours' back yard and entering through the back door which had been left open. The house was the same as his own, but its plan reflected a mirror-image, so he had no difficulty in locating, then ascending the stairs – and then, taking the bass guitar by the neck, bludgeoning each of their thick selfish skulls in turn as they sat round on beanbags in the rehearsal room. Toppling the drum kit, Stuart took the drum sticks and poked one through each of the drummer's eyes as he lay, slumped, his head bleeding where the heavy wood of the instrument's body had split his cranium open, wide, before leaving the 'musicians' in a pool of their own blood, which was a lot more attractive than their music.

The next morning Stuart awoke punctually, but feeling tired yet again. He went to work. He came home. It was a hard day at the office. Same as any other, Stuart reflected as he turned the key and heard the Yale's snib lift in the front door of the modest mid-terrace he rented. The pattern continued, day after day for the next two weeks. Stuart did nothing, hoping thc noisc would go away, hoping that someone else would have the courage to confront the nuisance neighbours from hell. Unable to settle to anything on any given evening, Stuart found his nerves becoming increasingly frayed, and that his alcohol consumption truly rocketed. How long could he cope like this? He would either collapse under the stress or have a breakdown – and how that might manifest itself, he had no idea. He had no wish to find out, either.

Kill the drummer, he can't play

Kill the bass player, kill both bass players

Kill the 3x bass expansion unit

Kill the sexplayer….

When the weekend took the shape of a 11am-11pm racketathon, punctuated by half-hour lulls in which only the sound of the stereo was audible through the walls – which, by this time, seemed like blissful peace to the weary and headache-plagued Stuart Bateman, he resolved on Monday morning to phone the letting agents whose sign he had seen a few weeks previous. Monday morning couldn't come soon enough, for Corporation HQ had become a place of sedate tranquillity relative to the construction site audio infernality of his home. Stuaart hadn't appreciated quite how badly this protracted disturbance was affecting him until when, between instrument bashing sessions, it was quiet enough to play a record of his own and he realized he couldn't face anything particularly guitar-heavy. This limited his choice significantly, for, in a collection which numbered over 1,000 LPs, there were very few records or CDs that were not essentially guitar-based. And so he found himself, after much deliberation, plumping for Duran Duran's *Rio*, an album he had grown up with, its slick production standing against everything that the noise next door represented. Just as 'The Chauffeur' faded out, the bastard noise started up again, and so Stuart took his cue to go to the shops, wherein to purchase groceries and to stock up booze. This he duly did, and spent the remainder of the weekend attempting to anaesthetise himself against the high-volume discord coming from the other side of the wall. It didn't really help: the combination of excessive alcohol, sleep deprivation, stress, restlessness and the effects of low-frequency vibrations working at his stomach for lengthy spells of time simply made him feel sick. Very fucking sick.

Monday came, he called the letting agents. They'd write to the inconsiderate pests. Stuart assumed that the letter probably arrived on Wednesday, the day that the little shits decided to crank the volume up to 11 after removing all the furniture and carpets from the rehearsal room. Stuart knew this because the sound was much louder and much more heavily reverbed. And because there was a roll of carpet, a wardrobe and two drawer units in the back yard getting rained on. He peered out of the study window in despair. Why did no-one else do anything? Why had no-one complained, called the pigs, environmental health, anyone? And why did they do this and not think they might be pissing a lot of people off? While many Blairites would probably blame the freedom culture of the '60s for paving the way for such social decline, Stuart laid the blame squarely at the feet of the laissez-faire consumer capitalist culture promoted by the Thatcher era, the '80s yuppie explosion, which New Labour had done little to halt the prevailing tide of through the late nineties and early years of the new millennium, for it was this culture which promoted greed, selfishness and inconsiderateness.

Tuesday came and went, then Wednesday. Every day was a hard day at the office. Same as any other. Every day drained into the next. Stuart could feel himself losing grip on his sanity as each night he grew evermore uptight, pacing about the house, slugging down vodka, fists clenched, veins throbbing, temples glistening, teeth gritted and nails gnawed, seething and stressed to snap. As the days passed and the din continued unabated, shaking Stuart's floors and walls and banister, his ribs, his bones, his lungs, his heart, his spleen and his frayed nerves. Nerves like nylon, nerves like steel… time and again he envisioned himself going round there and beating the fuckers to a pulp, but knew he didn't have it in him. But then something clicked within him, and he ran down the stairs, screaming hoarse, out of the back door and into the yard. He picked up a few pebbles and lobbed them at the upstairs window of his neighbour's house in an attempt to get their attention. Three stones of incrementally large size later, the third hit with a crack he feared would damage the glass. But instead, the music stopped. The top portion of the window was open, and through it voices could easily be heard.

"What was that?"

"Dunno… eh"

"Wot? Uh? I din't 'ear anyfink."

"SHUTTHEFUCKUUUUUUUUUUUUUUUUUUUUUUUUUUUUUP!!" Stuart howled in anguish at the top of his lungs. He repeated his demand again, and again, until he felt his throat ripping and nodules popping on his vocal chords.

One of the dumbasses appeared at the window.

"Fuck's sake, man, what's your fuckin' problem?" he snorted.

""Twat," muttered another one and spat out of the window, missing Stuart by a country mile.

They receded from the window and closed the open pane before resuming the sonic torture.

***

An hour later, all was quiet again. Stuart was soothing his throat with a neat vodka and reading from *The Portable Henry Rollins* when he heard a knock at the front door. He opened the door, but there was no-one there. Then he heard a splintering at the back door and raced to the other end of the house to find his back door being assaulted by a Converse-wearing foot which had just kicked in one of the panes. Another blow and the door was open. Standing in the doorway, Stuart looked up in time to see a 2"x4" full of rusty nails coming out of the blue and into his skull. Down, they proceeded to beat the living fuck out of him. Had he been conscious, he might have been amused by the irony that the gang of Nu-Metal louts were living out the fantasy he himself had repeatedly played out in reverse. Within minutes they had gone, vaulting back over the wall to their rented modest mid-terrace property with the broken furniture and torn carpets and yellowed curtains and gouged walls, leaving Stuart for dead, bleeding on his own back doorstep.

Barred

Bar scene: smoke hangs thick as voices rise and drift through the air. Bare oak beams support the wooden ceiling: the bar has the appearance, at least internally, of a barn, or an ancient aircraft hangar. Bare wooden floorboards are dirty, unvarnished, splintering, stained and sticky with ale spillage, phlegm, piss and vomit. Ash, cigarette butts and broken glass litter the boards, along with discarded crisp packets match boxes and spent rubbers.

Far end of the room: a long, mess-style wooden table on nailed-in trestles, long wooden benches running parallel up either length of the table. The era: 1989-94, the attire of the student types sitting at the long table provides the indication.

"Oasis. Yeah, love 'em. Rockin'," one average youth is saying loudly.

"Yeah. An' the Beatles, right," adds another guy in faded, baggy-cut blue denims, Nike trainers and an anorak.

"I reckon the Stone Roses really 'ad summink, y'know?" comes the contribution from another.

Close pan onto a guy at the end of the table on the corner of the bar. He is wearing a jelly-mould sun-hat pulled low, so as to partially obscure his eyes. The geezer has hair – masses and masses of unkempt, unwashed, bushy, dark, wavy hair. His monster sideburns are low-slung, meeting his fuzzed jawbone. They are bushy, frizzing out over his ears, encroaching over his cheeks in a lamb-chop figure. Where he has no sideburn, four days worth of dark, dense stubble covers his face. His hair reaches his shoulders and covers his anorak's collar and the huge wings of his shirt collars. The 30" flares say '70s throwback copyist retro motherfucker'. He stares straight ahead into the camera as it zooms in on his hairiness, and in a deep Mancunian monotone simply issues forth a single word:

"Man."

***

Cut to the other side of the bar. It's been a difficult day at the agency. Two men are deep in conversation. Their gesticulations indicate a great deal of passionate involvement in their subject matter, and that this is no regular barroom beer and football ramble.

The man on the left takes a large slug from his JD over ice. He is tall. Very tall, and lean. His hair is spiked and on his chin is a metaller's goatee tuft. His sharp features bear a very earnest expression, and his spindly metaller's moustache twitches occasionally as he emphasises each point with the utmost of care and deliberation.

"I think there are two modes of plagiarism which are acceptable…" he continued.

"…even if not wholly legitimate," his cohort interjected by way of concluding the point.

"Needless to say," he conceded with a nod of arrogance, "plagiarism and legitimacy aren't really in the same field. That's not my point here, as I think you well know. But what I am saying is that it's okay to plagiarise under certain circumstances, of which there are two:

"Either you're so sneaky about what you're nicking that it just doesn't ever get noticed by anyone ever, which is pretty damn cool, or you're so blatant with it, acknowledging sources all over the place, so that people actually get in on it and play with the piece, consciously looking all the time, combing through, to see if they can tell what's been lifted and from where."

"Elastica-style," offered the second man. He was considerably shorter, but no less lean. His hair was also short, but his face was clean shaven. A private detective with a penchant for cult literature, Bill Chunder was a highly literate character. The bar may well have been the seediest dive in this town, overpopulated by students and other miscellaneous dosser types, but the clientele provided him with a constant source of inspiration and light relief. When assignments were few, he'd concentrate his efforts on writing. As yet unpublished, he believed he had what it takes. Yes, the literary world really did need more hard-boiled detective fiction, and he was ready to prove it. Dashiel Hammett? Step aside, here's Bill Chunder…

The tall guy nodded.

"Maybe you're right," Bill conceded as he downed the last of his pint. He sat, thoughtfully, glancing about the smoggy bar. "So…" He lit a cigarette and drew hard. The tip glowed red and the paper receded toward his mouth. Smoke rose from the growing length of ash and spilled from his mouth as he spoke. How he loved that image. "Not much been doing down at the office, eh, Roger?"

Roger wasn't listening. Instead, he was casting a baleful eye over the students in the corner.

"Students," he spat with heavy distain.

"Mmm?"

"I hate fucking students."

"Hmmm… but…"

"All of them. The thing is, you *can* hate them collectively, because they're not individuals, and they're all so fucking smug. And what have they got to be smug about? 'Oh, I'm SOOO stressed! I've got 500 words to write by next month.' And then they finish up and go and temp as data inputters. What the hell have they got to be so fucking smug about? Nothing! I mean, look at that fuckwit in the corner."

"Sun-hat dude?"

"Yeah. I mean, I like living in a culturally diverse society, I really do, blah, blah, blah, and all that, but how can he be there in his sun-hat and flares and be so smug about everything? I mean, he actually thinks he's cool looking like that. And he thinks he's, like, original or something. And his body language tells me that he's smug about that…I mean, for fuck's sake…!"

Bill nodded. Roger had a daily rant about students. Not that he actually minded. He was hardly the biggest fan of the student stereotype himself. But when Roger started his daily anti-student tirade…well, you just have to let him go. He looked at the tall guy across the table. He was draining the remaining Jack Daniel's from the glass and pulling a 'sour' face. Roger was, like Bill, a private detective and part-time writer of hard-hitting crime fiction, also as yet unpublished. He was tall. He was lean. He was Roger Gash. He was hard-boiled. He was THE hard-boiled dick.

"I want to change my name," opined Bill whistfully.

"Why?" asked Roger flatly.

"Because I feel like a comedy character from a spoof '70s cop show. I think it's bad for business, Roger, that's why."

"But you are a comedy character," asserted Roger. "There's no escape. And do you really think I like my name? I've tried to change it. I wound up doing a few bit-parts with different names, but they were all equally ludicrous. I had a spell as a soldier, but Colonel Quim just can't command respect from a bunch of military poufters. Jim Twat the architect…he was dull…and do you think I actually enjoyed being cast as a labourer? Brickies just aren't sympathetic to a guy like Mark Muff. Look, I'm consigned to being a terminal cunt. And as for the kind of deals Rick Scrotum gets…"

"Bollocks!"

“Yeah, okay, so I made him up, but my point stands. At least you only have the mild impedance of coming over as a carsick lightweight…”

“Cunt.”

“…and he’s so smug looking! Up himself? I can’t see his fucking torso!”

“So anything much doing at the office?”

“A bit, Bill, a bit,” replied Roger.

“Do tell.”

“Well, first off, did I tell you they’d busted the 2D Kid?”

“No…”

“Yeah. Hauled his ass in yesterday. Turned out it was all a front.”

“No shit?”

“Nope. Absolutely no fucking shit. Straight up.”

“Christ.”

“And today…woah, we had some pretty fucking hardcore torture going down in the Shit Street lockups. Some mean-assed motherfucker with a grudge against some dude who dicked his bitch… Get this: the dude who’s chick had been doin’ the cheatin’ tattooed a life-size manta ray into his rival’s chest using a blunt razorblade. He incorporated the nipples to be the eyes, right, and he did this tattoo before removing the nipples with a pair of garden sheers. While he was still in shock over the tattooing and loss of both nipples, ‘capped him with a crowbar. Course, then he couldn't move, 'cause his hands were tied and his kneecaps out, so he was unable to defend himself against having a cheese grater applied to his scrotum and his penis sliced in two longways like a banana split with a machete..."

"That's brutal."

"Clinical."

"No shit."

"Yeah. Guy passed out. Brought him to with a monster shot of adrenaline before they finished him off - get this - by being disemboweled with a chainsaw...then they dismembered the corpse with a Stanley knife and pinned 2" square chunks of diced flesh to every wanted poster for the Harlem Hardnut in 3 states."

"No shit?"

"No shit. Straight up."

"Shit."

"No."

***

Cut to two girls at a table by the bar entrance.

"Who are those two guys over there?" asked the tall brunette of her blonde friend.

"Those guys there? That's Bill Chunder and Roger Gash," replied the blonde.

"Funny names. They sound like dodgy '70s cops…."

"They are. Well, they're private detectives, actually."

"…and they look like a couple of twats."

"True, but actually it's only the tall one who's really a twat. But I hear they're quite good…"

"Yeah. Useful…they're hired…"

Spliced

Steve's head was a mess. For once, it wasn't a hangover. Too long now, too long spent strung out, overworked, underpaid, oversocial, undersleeping, overdrinking, undersleeping: over time these things had begun to take their toll. But mostly he blamed his job. Their demands were unreasonable, but he had little option but to do as he was coerced or quit. With mounting debts – credit cards, loans, student loans, various tabs – plus overdue bills, quitting wasn't an option. And the long hours that were being forced upon him due to immense workloads – the result of yet another 'downsizing' project – meant that trawling the classifieds and completing applications for other jobs was, essentially, out of the question.

It was Sunday afternoon, a few hours before Steve's most hated time of the week. Even worse than Monday morning. Arriving at the office on a Monday morning, the worker is reunited with all the other corporate cocksuckers who have no choice either. They're all failures, but that's fine. The ones who are successful, who 'make it' in the industry and climb the corporate ladder, they're scum, and Steve had no wish to be like them. He wouldn't lower himself. What rankled was the fact that so many of those who seek and attain promotion do so undeservedly. Success is rarely an indicator of an individual's greatness, ability or skill. Moreover, quite the opposite is true. The corporate climbers are, generally speaking, wholly inept in social or job-applicable terms. They are, however, quite adept at self promotion, usually at the expense of others. If everyone else looks bad, then they, by comparison, positively shine. Survival of the shittest.

All of this hits the worker on Monday morning, and there's no escape. But Sunday nights were far worse, Steve maintained, because they were generally wasted in cold, fevered anticipation of the hell that was to come on the other side of sleep. But right now couldn't think of anything, at least not coherently. Thoughts all jostled, in no particular order, to become the leading thought, the one that led the train. Trying to clear his mind, Steve moved a chair over to the window and gathered a book from the shelf. He longed to escape, but as long as escape remained impractical, he could rely on books to provide some temporary escape, some small respite from the grim reality of his going-nowhere life. Few of the titles he owned were obvious 'escape' texts: he abhorred fantasy and horror, and, in the main, could not stand science fiction, with perhaps the notable exception of The Hitch-Hiker's Guide to the Galaxy, which was as much an exception in its own right anyway. Fundamentally, genre fiction left him cold. He instead preferred to immerse himself in works which, while still deeply involved with the human condition, did so in a way which enabled him to lose himself in the words, marveling at the quality of the prose, the startling or awe-inspiring turn of phrase. Having picked Martin Amis' *Money* for his latest piece of light entertainment, Steven realized after half an hour that he had read only two pages and had instead spent the time gazing out of the window listening to the mutter line of his own contradictory thoughts.

I pass another afternoon by the window. I watch people and cars pass, going about their business. What is their business? Business, always business. We never refer to people as going about their daily pleasure. Do they have daily pleasure, daily pleasures? Perhaps, perhaps not. But they go about their business in public, while they go about their pleasures in private. Me, I have neither business nor pleasure to attend to. Without money, in the world, I don't exist. I watch the world. Of course, it isn't the world, so much as the most minute microcosm. Of course, those who I see pass on the street below, they think it is the world. The world is what they make it, the world that they've shaped. The world revolves around them. To them, there is no world 'outside.' The whole world will come to them. They work, they earn their money, they take their foreign holidays and travel 'to see the world.' Except, of course, they don't. They see only the very smallest of postcard pictures of the world.

He focussed his mind in passing on an email he had received from a friend of his whom he no longer saw very often, in which he had outlined a new job he had landed.

The job sounds like a bit of a turkey, but the perks make like adequate compensation. It pays the bills and you'll get to shut the door when you're tossing off under the desk this time. And no-one'll be able to see when you're hacking. Smart move, office boy.

His friend had also suggested Steve should seek alternative employment, as his current job appeared to be killing him. His friend was right. But the very thought of going through the process of apply / interview / same shit different office sent waves of panic through his fragile system. Once again, his neural network began to twitch while his brain's circuits sent streams of unconnected signals across one another. Why…?

I think I can answer your perplexing lay drains into the next... 'simple' is the people you work with; 'eay drain into the next...

…cut-ups make explicit a psychosensory process that is going on all the time anyway. Somebody is reading a newspaper, and his eye follows the columns in the proper Aristotelian manner, one idea and sentence at a time. But subliminally he is reading the columns on either side and is aware of the person sitting next to him.

…started rubbing her tits against your drains into the next bra. Life, the workless wilderness, was beginning, the mind conceive, as far as the mind's eye... On the subject of definitions, it has pass in all directions, as much without start as afternoon. Okay, I dig completely why the though I had fallen into some kind of bad shit. I'm down with tha'. But what does cone present, with no points of reference on the says he must be stopped, that he cannot getting any younger, while all around me, definition of 'democracy.' Fascist he may so much as left the flat, I was reminded at democratically elected fascist, and true to napping my heals were. And how young I'm wrong of course, but... simple fact I eat shirts, not even conceived at the time of the job. Sounds like a bit of a turkey, but have developed hormones, let alone a need to... It pays the bills and you'll get to shut the e next week, be embarking on their degree this time. And no-one'll be able to see who Industrial Management, Public Relations.... kids, not yet halfway to adulthood, assessing. And yes, you are, most definitely, official – peers and those marginally younger than Rock Metal, indeed. Almost as uncool asking out their blind raging angst against the shan't even start on P.O.D. tonight. Christir parents not to give them enough pocket money do you still have your 'beard'? trainers... and by Christmas, they'd be certificates from some obscure former Hint: spend some of your hard-earned parents bought them for their graduations, 'Things to Do With a Dead Princess.' Her jobs, while the no-longer-up-and-coming any thirties are rejected out of hand by I have to remove lint from my authentic ie... pubescent sproglings, job applications dude. Human resources staff and personnel peoples, dismissed as past it, used up, obsolete, make it, compulsory retirement must surely heap of life. Bled dry by the system, their withering and crisping, the crackling cadavers.

His mind momentarily settled on another recollection long enough to steady his grasp of time and place, and he slowly replayed, for the umpteenth time, his last pay review with his manager.

Walk into meeting room. Sit down. He presents Steve with his productivity figures for August through to November inclusive (August 108%, Sept 101%, Oct 99%, Nov 103%), and says "Consistent… what do you make of those?"

"Pretty good," Steve replies. What else can he say? He's averaging in excess of 100% target productivity for the last third of a year.

"Some people are making 150%. What do you say to that?"

"Great."

"So why aren't you, if other people can do it?"

Depends on their standard of work and what work they get on a daily basis, Steve tells him this.

"I think it's because the recommended times for tasks are far too generous. 6 minutes for a task is generous: it must be if people are doing them quicker."

"Times are based on AVERAGES. I take average time to do stuff. So what? I think the times are fair," Steve tells him.

"I think you're wrong."

And so it continues: a 45-minute panning for meeting targets and failing to exceed them. Steve has replayed this script, this roll of mental film over and over, and it's starting to become grainy and crackly, but the dialogue is always the same. Why did this come to mind in the here and now? Steve wondered, but this ponderance was swiftly answered when he remembered his next review is imminent, a mere three days away. He needed something…an angle, a miracle…

If journalists designed laptops, things would be a little different. Portable computers would never be any wider or taller than an 8 1/2-by-11 sheet of paper, since we don't have that much extra room in our luggage.

Steve needed a drink.

"…he's not always drunk…"

"Was he loud when you go there?"

"He's in a cul-de-sac, and he wasn't there, and… yeah…"

"…yeah, yeah…"

"Yeah…"

Steve had to get out of the house. He pulled on his coat in a daze, not knowing where he would go. But he will call on the helmet, consider this, up into a pub and a puff of if of a modern pub over the joys of experimental writing don't we just love it you breathe and it right's new farce and its types. The miracles of modern technology – pace around and I can write tosh, it has a right… checked himself, the man walking to bark out size. The night was dark cold.

"Gimme a beer" he barked at the barman. The barman turned looking up-and-down, and sneered in Steve's face.

"Yeah? Ordeal want to?" the phrase was unclear.

"What do you want?" asked another man standing at the bar to Steve's left, while indicating toward the barman. Was this an offer?

Steve was appalled at the barman as poor diction. "I want a beer," he said evenly.

"Yeah?" said the barman

"yeah," replied Steve

"you think are you one that served you?" Sneered at the barman.

Already confused, Steve found the barman's crypticism bewildering and glanced around uneasily. The room was almost empty and the background was fading into cigarette smoke.

"I don't see a great many other people here to give you business," Steve said.

The barman turned away and walked further back further down the bar …corrective phase bar, shifting now, dreamscape of a warping memory. With a damp cloth, he turned to the spirits counter and picked up a packet of cigarettes. He opened the packet of and took out a cigarette. She put a cigarette to his lips. Taking a box of matches from his back pocket he struck a match and lit a cigarette. He inhaled deeply and, and blow up a large puff of smoke across the bar.

Stephen watched the bombings actions with the rising irritation. "Hey you!"

The barman turned and looked at Steve. "Yeah?" He looked at Steve as though Steve worked in the wrong.

"Do I get a beer?" Steve frowned. His first and to meet for beer was beginning to get to him. He didn't meet hassle from a cunt like this a time like this.

But enough of Marseilles in this is none the less this number anything bars and pubs and accounts do mean shades when you're talking about new random voice activating knowledge leaf and the future of literature and the Neath off the street he tastes run very.

Once served with drink, Steve found himself a table in a darkened corner. The evidence was everywhere. His life was a fading, crumbling artefact, the historical details ingrained like age-stains, or otherwise collected like housedust in the unswept corners. The world kept moving, kept on turning, but somehow, somewhere, at some point, some time, he felt that he had halted. Times change. The world these 15-year old inhabited, so very different from that of the generation before, even the decade before… at what point innocence lost now? Years before 15, years before the realization of body image that comes with puberty and the dawning of physical maturity. From those first steps, family snaps of Jennie's first Gap Kids jeans, Jamie's first Burberry baseball cap and before even that, the Versace babygrow, the Gucci carrycot mum used to carry her precious cargo in to 'do lunch' with the girls… plush pizzeria, white whine spritzers out of favour to Bacardi Breezers, the choice of a new generation of hip young twenty-something / thirty-something mothers.

He glanced around, and covertly cocked an ear to the conversations about him.

"The St. tastes for Rank – ahem, who face - yes who face indeed. Come. Phosphate. Tracc sniff becomes phosphate account becomes your income."

"Bli'me," to the editing the riders meet the ranting 22 pacing about "what do I need?"

"To wave and ambient light around the overseeing what the FA turns up to date slut mighty very loudly to limes Jesse flattened."

"Is correcting cheating a fall?"

"Cheerful mainly! Moreover, cheating a fool."

When we do crank up the tally Co excess yep ago for a minor factor whom would from from her behave how. My horror per month for you like phosphates question mark you are like phosphate? Yeah I love the fuckers just like I love the jewel in of the Nile. 'Ow you go around it: this means clever you wanna take the right to rest of writing? Then learn how to underwrite. How underwrites? Underwrite? Don't talk to me about underwriting. This it's that kind of shit that got me here in the first place. Her, there and not every where. If…

More empty conversations provided the soundtrack to Steve's inchoate mental meanderings as he sat and stared gloomily through his pint of Specked Hen and recalled a novel he had read some years before. In it lay the implicit idea that everyone is a lit-groupie of sorts: everyone is writing a book. Gadge into a party and tell people you're an insurance broker, and people will either ask for advice or switch off – more often than not the latter. Tell them you're a writer, and they're all ears. 'You're a writer?' or 'You're writing a novel? Wow. It's funny you should be doing that; I'm actually writing a novel too.' If you're really unlucky, and particularly drunk, you might find you've given out your email address to one or more of these prats, and soon enough, samples of their shitty shorts and piss-poor prose passages start streaming into your inbox. Such incomings would be cheering, even downright hilarious, were it not for the fact that it's these socialite illiterates that invariably end up getting published – 'My uncle has a friend in publishing, don't you know? He put a good word in for me…' And would he put a good word in for me, too? 'Of course.' Yeah, right. Funny how they manage to continually forget, how they never have time for the rank outsider. They're so slippery and elusive, these 'contacts' people. The moral of the book, then, if it indeed had one, was 'be careful to whom you reveal your literary aspirations.' Taking another sip from the glass, he lamented that he was, now, seemingly alone in the world. Worst of all, instead of being surrounded by closet wannabe novelists, he was surrounded by pseuds whose sole desire was to claim fame by proxy. Everyone knew Damien Hurst. And for the less imaginative still, there was the evermore intricate / irritating (delete as appropriate) ringtone, the evermore compact mobile phone, the ever-baggier trouser, the evermore powerful computer. And it had to be a Mac, lest we forget.

The question resurfaced: which horse? Horse? Be much more. Bitch whore. Slag in band could. Indeed. See back in of the ban it ran it up your marks and sack the to do retire here?!!.... Punctuation indeed. Once had the dictation device has mastered the art of Prof., you have got it cracked, the motherfuckers. Except excepted exceed exit. French you. Thank you. Catch cack-handed crack at and van one of of-of were at the pub and Peru ambient sounds take on new meaning as. But how would does one interpret these and sound? Or boiling the air Pueblo. Problems.

Silly question mark. On our air.

He said: "They said murder. I asked them who they had murdered and they said some kid in Peckham."

The scientists said the drug tells the body's muscles to burn off carbohydrate and fats and prevents them from being stored in fat tissue.

Steve was tired, bone tired, deliriously tired. Day / night, real / reflection, arse / elbow, it was impossible to discern and he cared even less. All the faces, all the voices blurred and changed to one face, changed to one voice. One day he would recall all of this and recount it in some form or another, cogently, coherently, lucidly, and in his own words – your very own words, indeed! And who are you? Yes, one day he would make sense of it all. But for now, he would simply have another drink and try to distance his mind ceaseless, screaming from his exhaustion-wracked body. If only he could sleep… perchance to dream….

Recent studies of dream and sleep have yielded a wealth of data that was not available in Freud's day. Perhaps the most important discovery is the fact the dreams are a biological necessity. Deprived of REM sleep, experimental subjects show all symptoms of sleeplessness, no latter how much dreamless sleep they are allowed. They become irritable and restless and experience hallucinations. No doubt prolonged deprivation would result in death.

He's in a cul-de-sac… the beginning is also the end.

Scum

I had time to kill. And so I wandered. To call my activity 'wandering the streets' would have been rather misleading. But I did have some time to kill before my train was due and I figured the best way to pass that time was in a pub, wherein I could sit and read my book in peace, accompanied by a pint or two. But I'm a fussy drinker and not such a fussy dresser. I look out of place in those trendy wine-bar type places. Besides, they rarely sell proper beer, instead catering for the lowest-common-denominator market with their electrically-pumped overpriced pissy lager chilled to some unnatural sub-zero temperature at which your lips stick to the glass and your bladder contracts in shock the moment the hyperchilled fluid hits your gullet.

And so I wandered aimlessly – or almost aimlessly – in search of an appealing-looking hostelry. Time was when the streets would have been lined with proper drinking taverns, dark, smoke-filled and yet somehow welcoming as places one could hunker down with a beer, rest one's feet and mind or hide away from the outside.

Finally, I installed myself with my pint of mild and got my book out. Bukowski always made a good travelling companion.

A tap on my shoulder. “Excuse me, young man, you’re in my seat.”

Without turning I clambered down from the usurped bar stool and gathered my bag, repositioning myself at the bar with my book.

“Sorry, I didn’t know you were there.” I thought you’d left.

Without replying, the phlegmatic old cunt recovered his stool, dragging it back to its previous position in front of the cigarette machine and about six feet away from the bar itself. The old bastard coughed, a loose, hacky cough, as he clambered aboard, then lit a roll-up.

As I recovered my place in *South of No North*, still a little flushed with embarrassment and unease at the exchange and finding myself to be the sole person standing and drinking at the bar, I noticed a sign before me which read ‘no smoking at the bar. Thankyou.’ That explained why the old duffer had situated his stool there, then. Presumably the six feet represented an agreed ‘safe’ distance from the bar at which one could chuff. My feet ached. My mild was too cold and a little gassy, not to mention a little bland. But it went down well enough and quickly enough to enable me to finish reading a three-page short and make a swift exit. Back in the street, the dazzling daylight stung my eyes. What now? More aimless wandering? I decided to cut my losses and head to the train station – not a particularly inspiring or restful place to while away the hours, but at least there was little chance of missing my train if I was already there almost an hour early.

As I made my way to the station, I found the streets lined not with the noble poor or bums trying to pick a living from the bins and the gutters, but seething masses of the ignoble rich, wannabe rich and would-have-you-believe-they're rich. I had to wade through a crowd of kids to enter the station. It was past lunchtime, and their school uniforms suggested they should have been elsewhere. Instead, they hung about, all fags 'n' chuddy, the boys with their baseball caps pulled down low and their jeans and tracksuit bottoms even lower, the girls with their large hooped earrings, ties knotted short, blouses loose and miniskirts tight against roughly-shaven sausagey thighs "'Ere, can yer crash us a fag?"

"Fook off"

"'Ere, mister…"

"You fuckin' startin'?"

"I aren't bothered."

"Me neiver…"

A few points and hushed snickers, perhaps, but I slipped past them almost unnoticed for a change, willing myself the ability to exist if only temporarily as *el hombre invisible*… I had made it to the station unscathed.

The platforms were clogged with them. Not school children, but them in general. The scum of the earth: people. An obese teenager pushing a pram, cigarette in the one hand, guiding the child's buggy, mobile phone in the other, raised to her ear.

"'Cause", she bellows with a coarse swagger, "it wan't me 'oo went thru' customs wi'r an 'arf up me snatch!"

Skip forward five years, the only dope-smoking year one sits in the playground, her knees too weak to support her enormous frame. The other kids point and laugh, for despite their own obesity, little Chardonnay who ain't so little remains something that must be beheld, marvelled at, ridiculed.

"Wot you lookin' at?" she yells at the closest gawping fat kid. "Come 'ere and I'll kick yer in the snatch."

"I just want to be your friend."

"Yeah? Got any blow?"

Back in present time, another mother, this time dragging a toddler by her side as she waddles to and fro, her flip-flops flapping against the yellowing soles of her feet, crosses my line of vision.

"Nathan! Shut up, or I'm going to smack you so hard…." She bawls at the child who is in turn bawling, its face red and chocolate-smeared, its fists clenched and also covered with the same sticky brown gunk that is slaumed not just on its face but also its clothes. The threat just brings more intense, raw-throated fraught wailing and a new intensity of combined anger and anguish to the flow of tears and snot, the reward for which is a sharp blow to the buttocks, with the inverse of the desired effect. "I fuckin' warned you!"

Businessmen, everywhere, crawling like ants or rats across the concrete concourses, scurrying between the shops and vending machines, clutching briefcases, mobile phones and overpriced coffees with the flavour of mud housed in plastic-lidded cardboard beakers.

"Yeah... yeah... tell Phil I need those figures by 10am tomorrow," a flash git in a grey pinstripe suit hardballs into his mobile telephone the size of a matchbox and he breezes past me.

"I'll ring through with the stats when I'm on the train," another voice swerves from behind me. He passes me, then halts abruptly to check his watch, check the departures board and then his watch again. He is wearing designer glasses, his hair his gelled to a perfectly coifed flick upwards at the front. He is using his mobile on a hands-free set, which leaves him able to cart his laptop bag and briefcase about freely. "Yeah, yeah, I have them. I've got them with me, but I need to get into my briefcase and I'm just on the platform waiting for my train... it should be here any minute. Yeah. Yeah. Er... yeah, yeah yeah. Right, ok, I'll talk to you shortly, mate. Alright, yeah. Ok." He looks around, a look of panic in his eyes.

An announcement comes on over the tannoy, and after another glance at his watch and the departures board, he's off, at a jog, up the stairs two at a time, appearing on the opposite platform just as the train pulls away... I watch him, amused. He's back on his mobile again, although this time he's beyond the range of my hearing.

The platform was becoming crowded following a near-subliminal influx of suits. A mobile phone rang and sent everyone rummaging through their bags and pockets. A barrel-chested businessman took the call and began to belt out instructions, projections, measurements and directions.

"Yeh. Tell John he needs to get onto Andy about the contractor's quote. Yeh. He's got all the details down..."

He paced up and down the platform, twelve paces forth, twelve paces back, a pudgy finger upon the hand which did not hold the receiver, crooked yet half-pointing, was brought down at around chest height as though punctuating the close of each sentence or independent clause. “Yeh. Call Steven Thompson right away:” *(finger)* “get him to make the reservations.” *(finger)* “Club class flights for all of us.” *(finger)* “Yeh. From Gatwick.” *(finger)*

He was wearing a double-breasted suit, fastened and straining around the girth of his midriff. The ensemble also featured a grey shirt with fasten-down collars and a garish tie and was accessorized with brown brogues. Brown brogues! I’m no fashion guru by any stretch of the imagination, and nor have I the means to be hip with it even if I did have the inclination, which, of course, I don’t. However, at least I know bad attire when I see it, and suffice to say, sir, that brown brogues are a serious style faux-pas in any circle. Always have been, and one would suspect, always will be. Especially in a ‘business’ context. Especially when the wearer’s clearly trying to look chic, monsieur. Really, the only people who can even get close to getting away with brown brogues are academics, of the tweedy variety. Brown brogues are an acceptable accessory to, say, a tweed jacket and trousers combo (if you really must), or a brown corduroy and cream or mustard cable-knit sweater getup. Yes, the jacket will ideally have leather, split hide or suede(ette) elbow pads. At least in this setting, the brown brogues compliment the rustic / eccentric look. At least the kind of people who dress in this way aren’t out to impress, and if they do have designs on being impressive, it’s for their academic prowess, rather than their presentation and corporate marketability.

My train pulls in and I board. Most of the seats are occupied by lone travellers, but none of whom I fancy sharing my journey with. Some make it quite obvious that they do not want the 'spare' seat to be taken by some random stranger by placing bags, coats, books or various other personal belongings in the space. So territorial: 'this is mine.' Unless you have two arses, you only need one seat, but I do understand the traveller's wish to avoid being hemmed in by some smelly, sweaty fidgety tossbag who spends the duration of the ride with dance music or lamecore shit-hop bleeding from their headphones at PA volume, breaking only to bawl into their phone about what they got up to the night before.

"Yeah, it was wicked. I was fookin' mashed, hurhurhur! Did yer see Jonesey? Yeah, when 'ee came out of the 'ospital. 'Is shoulder's bust, hurhurhurhurhurhurhur!"

I bypassed the occupied seats, the 'don't sit here' seats, the reserved seats, the seats taken by middle-aged, middle-England women with middle-class aspirations as they poured over their Sudoku puzzle books rested upon a strategically-placed copy of the *Daily Mail*.

I managed to find an empty seat and slid myself into position, just ahead of a deluge of Oxbridge-type students all wearing tweed jackets and woolen scarves, lugging huge rucksacks and instrument cases down the carriage aisle.

"Mahst be seats for Durham hyaah!"

"Yah. Jast keep going a little further, Piers."

As they ponced up and down the carriages in search of their apparently non-existent seats, accusations of double-booking and demands for a compensatory switch to first class were toffed about with increasing frequency and aggravation.

"No, if we'hh not able to be provided with ahh reservations, they mast put ahs into first clahrse," one toffee-nosed tithead in a mauve velvet blazer spiffed.

"Oh, absolutely," a snake-belted inbred spastic lolled in a tone which dripped caviar.

It took them until after the train had pulled out to get to the end of the carriage and I just knew I'd not seen the last of them.

I glanced about me to discover that the two sets of tables, in front of and cross-aisle from my seat were occupied by a collective of business delegates. They were removing their jackets and rolling the sleeves of their shirts, some of which were striped, others of which were in pastel shades with white collars. So last century. Some of them were unveiling their laptops, while other piled their Filofaxes on the tables before them. Every last one of them had their mobile phone either in their hand or in front of them. The older ones were talking across one another, vying for the position of alpha male. They all nodded vigorously as they made cases in the most vociferous of terms, proffering forth the pros and cons of various locations, budget plans and which person would be best suited to which position. It was all meaningless, and I deduced that subconsciously some of them knew it. But they weren't going to give it up, as this was their life. Cross-aisle from me sat a balding man in his late forties. He had a convex face, which sloped down from his forehead into a hooked proboscis of gargantuan proportions and dominated his facial landscape which sloped away into a weak mouth and almost non-existent chin. Glancing through his spectacles at the open Filofax before him, it must have occurred to him how empty his week, and, by association his life was. I was able to make out the entries for each day of the week:

Wednesday: meeting 1-2, 3-4.

Thursday:

Friday: Charity dress-down

He picked up his pen and scribbled something in for Wednesday before picking up his mobile and dialling up someone, anyone, who would talk to him and make him look important, or at least busy.

"Hi… Dave? It's Nigel here…"

The younger ones, too were immersed in business-related topics of conversation, all desperately trying to prove themselves worthy, and to show to their elders that they should be their next in line, throwing out the corporate speak at nineteen to the dozen.

"Until that time… I just feel as though I'm one of the girarffes…" The Southern elongation of the second syllable of the word 'giraffe' stood out above the gruff, broad-vowelled intonations of his more northern colleagues even more than the strangeness of the analogy being made.

"Do you know what kind of utilities they've got in place for this project? I hear Jack Nosegay's the project manager, and then when it's done he's going to step aside for Matt Beckham to take the role of Head Of."

"I'd heard that too, but I was speaking to Steve Swinton and he was saying that Matt might manage the project and then stay on."

"Ooh… I think it's a really interesting project. But it's been really hard to move forward on until now because in the early stages it was… well, there was a lot of chefs on it and it was hard to make headway. But now we're starting to capture the soft knowledge and people are starting to buy into it more. I just hope we get to move quite quickly now."

"Me too. It's such a great building."

"Oh yeah, it's so much better… it's awesome, innit?"

"Do you know where your desk is?"

"Not yet…"

Feeling nauseous I buried my head in the Bukowski until the train pulled in at my station. I disembarked, although not without difficulty. A clamour of thickwits wanting to board the train hadn't the sense to let passengers off before trying to wrestle their way on, thrusting suitcases and rucksacks up the step and against my shins the moment I opened the door.

The smell of chocolate with a minty undercurrent met my nostrils as my feet met with the pavement. The batch of confection being produced marked a change from that rolling off the conveyor belt that morning as I had made my way toward the station: then, my sense of smell had been pleasured by the aroma of chocolate with a caramelly undercurrent. It was hard to decide which I preferred, although I reminded myself that it mattered little: production of chocolate here would soon cease as the lines were due to be closed in favour of large new factories on the mainland, with more modern machines and a cheaper workforce. Ultimately, it all comes down to economics: fuck a century and a half's chocolate-making tradition and a small city's employment levels, it's money that counts. There's no room for emotion or sentimentality. The shareholders don't get dividends in compassion.

I turned a corner and the breeze carried a different aroma in the form of the sickly-sweet earthy smell of sugar beet. That too would soon be gone as the beet factory was scheduled for closure, with the loss of several hundred jobs, if one considered the associated growers, hauliers, etc., who also relied on the processing of this popular crop, although British production was becoming, like everything else, threatened by cheaper imported goods. Factory smog was once a sign of progress…. Casting these thoughts from my mind I continues to make my way homewards.

There was simply no escaping them. Passed by a school, the noise of children thronging in my ears. Children, abandoned by their parents and coming a close second to work sit stone-faced as they pass in taxis their surly demeanours set in imitation of their perpetually grizzly mothers. Other mothers who have made the time or effort to turn out to collect their offspring stand in clusters, straddling the pavement and blocking it to regular pedestrians who have somewhere to go and aren't only using the footpath as a runway between school and SUV beefing vociferously about the cost of shoes and school clothes in an attempt to justify their working lives to the mothers who stand around in cardigans and sandals, making like their kids are their priority and they're willing to sacrifice career and working for the man in favour of some hippie ideal while their husbands work for IBM and arrive home in the BMW to readymade by M&S dinner on the table. And their lives were just so much better, and they wanted to make sure everyone knew it. But such displays of one-upmanship had to be conveyed subtly, of course, there could be no literal climbing on the shoulders of the others and tugging at the hair as they scrambled their way to the top of the social heap and its microcosmic reflection as stood on the peripheries of the playground, for that was no example to set the children.

"…Well, yes, John's working away a lot now so I'm having to do everything myself… he's involved in a major project. Yes, he's in energy…"

"Ooh, really?" *Must keep her talking: her husband's rich. Maybe we can be friends. Perhaps we'll get invited round for dinner. Maybe John's a mason and would be able to recommend my Alex…*

"Yes, yes…"

"It sounds fascinating." *Forced enthusiasm.*

"It is, I think, although he's very busy and travels a lot." *Brimming, gushing, the perfect opportunity to laud it over Janet what's-her-name who thinks she's so special in her D&G glasses and Armani jeans… fakes anyway by the looks of them. And I should know, I've got three pairs of genuine Aramani jeans in my wardrobe. They go so well with John's Armani jackets for those smart-casual events...* "And it's very difficult you know, trying to develop new stations and things with all these environmentalists protesting and getting in the way. Don't they realize they need power to run their dishwashers in 30 years time?"

"Oh dear, that's terrible," *Genuine concern now.* Janet loves her dishwasher, couldn't live without it, in fact. "I just don't get these dropout environmentalist types. They're just not seeing the bigger picture." *Finding common ground here...* "My Alex has the same sort of problem… he's in pharmaceuticals and has to fight his way past protesters just to get into the lab some mornings. These animal rights campaigners, they're so stupid. They don't seem to realise how all of their life-saving medicines and drugs come from or that they have to be tested for safety"

"I know, I know…" *Damn, clinical research... education, highly paid job with one of the major drugs companies perhaps... must try to fit in before knocking her down.* "I mean, they'd be the first to complain if there was no treatment for their families when they get cancer or leukemia or whatever. So short-sighted." *Good schpeel, but getting off-topic. Need to show her we're really better.* "So anyway, at least it's all in a good cause… I must dash, I've got to get to the travel agent's before they close."

"Ooh, are you off somewhere nice?"

Yes, she took the bait! "We're having a fortnight in …although me and the kids don't see as much of John as we'd like, we do at least get to spend some proper quality time on holiday… don't we, Joe? Yes, that's right, we get to go away to hot places with daddy!"

The ones who had already steered their rowdy spawn into their death machines were sitting stodgily behind the wheels, the fruits of their lard-coated loins placated with packets of crisps and brightly-coloured, gelatine-clogged, toxin-brimming sweets, all the better to rot your teeth with, my dear.

Finally I rounded the corner and into the street where I live. I fumbled to get my key into the lock, but with a waver, finally managed to slip the metal into the hole and with a sharp twist, unlatched the snib and threw the door open on my small but comfortable domain, my rented safe haven away from it all.

I raced through to the kitchen, slamming the front door behind me in a single deft move. Therein I grabbed a glass from the cupboard, a beer from the fridge and within moments had downed a good third of the drink. Ahh! I needed that… it was hot outside now and I was thirsty, and what's more I needed a mild anaesthetic to ease the pain of all that I had seen in the last three hours. The drink was going down well, refreshing the parts other drinks couldn't reach. As it slowly seeped through my tripwire-tense system, I headed upstairs to change.

Look out of the window... down below, on the street, a 2-seater BMW with soft-top and metallic blue finish slows and then stops. Doesn't pull over, just sits, engine humming in the way expensive motors do. Sounds the horn. Waits. 10 seconds... fifteen... girl of 18 or 19 pads down the steps from her front door in her Nike trainers and distressed designer denims. She has a striped scarf slung about her neck and over her shoulder, casual, is wearing a zip-fronted cardigan and is holding a metallic-effect foil-finish ring binder under her left arm. In her right hand she is clutching a patent leather handbag no bigger than the average purse. Don't need a large bag to carry credit cards in, dahling. Yeah, we're all impressed. Boyfriend has a BMW. Total fucking moron, shit in bed, but looks the part, drives the car, wears the clothes, walks the walk and is flash with the cash. Presents every weekend, free lifts to lectures and classes. Friends are all in awe, so, so jealous... Down on the pavement... group of three boys in Nike tracksuits and trainers dragging their feet along the damp black surface.

I am now wearing clean trousers, untainted by the grime of the other rail passengers, the fumes flooding from the cars and vans and tanks, the smell of sugar beet. My glass is empty. As I pour another beer, the silence of the empty house reverberates in my ears.

Flashback...

I turn to look and see the phlegmatic old cunt recovering his stool, dragging it back to its previous position in front of the cigarette machine and about six feet away from the bar itself. The old bastard coughs, a loose, hacky cough, as he clambers aboard, then lights a roll-up.

In the hallway I catch sight of my weary face in the mirror. I stop and look again. I look so *tired*. But there's something more… then the full horror hits me. I cough, that hacking, spluttering, sputum-rattling cough. Time for another roll-up, another pint…

How time flies when you're sleepwalking through life.

www.ingramcontent.com/pod-product-compliance
Ingram Content Group UK Ltd.
Pitfield, Milton Keynes, MK11 3LW, UK
UKHW041928190726
13854UKWH00004B/1505

9 781847 999795